She leant back against the door and Joss stood in front of her, filling her vision with the wide shoulders of his exquisitely cut suit.

'Everything okay?' he asked, his voice low and sensual.

Eva nodded, when what she really wanted to do was shout. To tell him that, no, she *wasn't* okay. This was far, far from okay. This was confusing and terrifying and oh, so much more complicated than she had ever wanted her life to be.

But she couldn't let go of his hand. Couldn't be the one to break that connection between them.

She'd felt it growing as they'd played their parts over dinner. The touch of a hand here. The brush of fingers over an arm there.

Intimacy had grown between them in some strange simulacrum of the relationship they had invented. But she had expected them to walk away from it. Expected to leave it at the table. She hadn't expected it to stalk them into the lift and back up to their suite.

Intimacy was safe in public, where neither of them could act on it. But with her back against this door and Joss in front of her—looking serious, smelling delicious—it was a more dangerous prospect. And Joss knew it too.

Dear Reader,

It is one of the great privileges and pleasures of being a writer that you get to live vicariously through your characters, and with Eva I've really gone to town. I've given her a talent and skill that I've always hankered after—she's a polyglot, speaking seven languages fluently and able to chat in several more. She has a glamorous job, working for a centuries-old chain of luxury department stores, and then I go and throw her a fake engagement to her gorgeous, enigmatic new boss. Really, what more could either of us want?

Of course there's more to Eva than just her glamorous job, and more to Joss than just that enigmatic smile, and it has been so much fun finding out more about them and their stories. I hope you enjoy stepping into Eva's shoes as much as I did.

Love,

Ellie

CONVENIENTLY ENGAGED TO THE BOSS

BY
ELLIE DARKINS

First Published in Great Britain 2017
By Mills & Boon, an imprint of HarperCollins*Publishers*
1 London Bridge Street, London, SE1 9GF

© 2017 Ellie Darkins

ISBN: 978-0-263-06973-0

Printed and bound in Great Britain
by CPI Antony Rowe, Chippenham, Wiltshire

Ellie Darkins spent her formative years devouring romance novels, and after completing her English degree decided to make a living from her love of books. As a writer and editor, she finds her work now entails dreaming up romantic proposals, hot dates with alpha males and trips to the past with dashing heroes. When she's not working she can usually be found running around after her toddler, volunteering at her local library or escaping all the above with a good book and a vanilla latte.

Books by Ellie Darkins

Mills & Boon Romance

Frozen Heart, Melting Kiss
Bound by a Baby Bump
Newborn on Her Doorstep
Holiday with the Mystery Italian
Falling for the Rebel Princess

Visit the Author Profile page at millsandboon.co.uk.

For Mike

CHAPTER ONE

'COULD YOU HELP me with this zip, or are you just going to watch?'

Instinctively Joss shut the door behind him, wondering if anyone else had seen, and glanced through the window of the office to make sure his father wasn't nearby.

'Sorry, Eva. I was looking for my dad. What are you doing in his office? And why does it involve being undressed?'

Eva shrugged—he watched her shoulder blades move under pale, exposed skin where the dress's zip was gaping at the back.

'Edward's already gone to the boardroom. Shouldn't you be there too? Never mind. Could you help? I should have been there five minutes ago, but I spilt a cup of coffee over myself and now I've got the zip stuck.'

'Okay, okay—sure,' Joss said, with a glance back at the closed door. 'My dad wanted to see me in here before the meeting, but I couldn't get away from my last call.'

He reached Eva and gently batted her hands away

from the zip, pulling the slider to the top as quickly and impersonally as he could manage.

Eva turned her head to look over her shoulder, and as his eyes met hers he felt the tug of attraction that was ever-present around his father's executive assistant.

'Um… Joss, I meant *un*zip.'

Oh, no, that was *not* what he'd signed up for. No way was he that stupid. He'd been keeping his eyes, hands and mind off this woman for years. He knew the limits of his self-control, and just this proximity to her was pushing it—never mind anything else.

'I'm not sure that's…'

'Joss, would you just do it? Shut your eyes, if you want, but get me out of this thing! It's not like I'm naked under here, in case you're worried about your delicate sensibilities.'

He took a deep breath and unzipped, but the teeth snagged halfway down her back.

'It's stuck.'

'Still? Brilliant. I was hoping it was just the angle I was pulling it. Can you unstick it?'

He wasn't sure he wanted to—not when unsticking it meant exposing more creamy skin and finding out exactly what she'd meant when she said that she wasn't naked under there.

Joss fiddled with the zip, passing the teeth slowly through the slider and unpicking the threads that had got caught. Finally it gave way and slid smoothly down Eva's back, revealing a silk slip in a soft pink colour, edged with delicate cream lace. Worse than naked, perhaps, to be so close to seeing the body that he'd dreamed of, only to find it tantalisingly out of reach.

'At last! Thank goodness for that,' Eva said, stepping quickly out of the dress and reaching for another, which Joss had just noticed draped over his father's chair. As the fabric was sliding over her head he turned for the door, but Eva stopped him. 'Wait—can you zip up this time? I don't want to be any later than I already am.'

Joss let out a sigh, but crossed the office again and reached for the slider of the zip, his fingertips very close to the rose silk at the base of her spine. He lingered for a moment as he swept her hair away with his other hand, revealing the wispy baby hairs at the nape of her neck and the invitingly soft skin behind her ear.

But before he could cover her safely, the door behind him opened.

'Eva, are you in—?'

Damn his father and his terrible timing.

'I'm sorry, Edward. I'll be right there,' Eva said, reaching for the zip herself and pulling it further down in the process of twisting round.

'No, no—I can see I'm interrupting,' Edward said. 'I trust you're both on your way.'

Joss couldn't bring himself to look, but he could almost *hear* the huge grin on his father's face, verging on a full-on laugh.

'We're waiting for you.'

His father left the room before Joss could explain that nothing had been going on between him and Eva. He shot a look at her, and saw she looked as taken aback as he did as she struggled with her dress. He pulled the zip up for her—no lingering this time—and strode for the door.

'What are we going—?' Eva started.

'I'll handle it,' Joss said.

He walked into the boardroom, still fighting images of Eva's lingerie-clad body and the look of intrigue and delight on his father's face when he'd so clearly misinterpreted what had been going on in his office.

He was more used to seeing disappointment from his father, especially when it involved him and women. Since Joss's first marriage had failed, his father had tried to hide his disappointment that he'd not been able to settle down with anyone else. He knew that when he'd first told his parents he was getting a divorce, they'd blamed the break-up on him.

And then, when he'd walked into the office as a single man, emerging from the dark clouds of clinical depression and divorce, he had realised the strength of his attraction to his father's executive assistant.

He'd told himself that he would not be going near her—under any circumstances. His father doted on her, and would not take kindly to her feelings being hurt. And after what Joss had done to his marriage—the destruction he'd been powerless to prevent—he knew that he couldn't expect to make any woman happy.

At least his father respected him professionally. He'd been working for the family's chain of luxury department stores since he was in primary school, and had earned his position as Vice President of UK Stores. But professional respect and personal pride were two very different things, and Joss knew that an abundance of one would never compensate for the lack of the other.

All eyes turned to him as he entered the full board-room, with Eva right behind him. They found a couple of spare chairs in the corner. Sunlight flooded in through the old lead-paned windows, brightening the panelled room, which could feel oppressive on a gloomier day.

Joss tried to catch his father's eye, but he was either deliberately avoiding his gaze or so entranced by the view out of the window that he couldn't bring himself to look away. The well-heeled streets of Kensington were bustling below, and Joss could tell just from the hum of the traffic that the pavement outside the store was filled with shoppers and tourists, stopping to take in the magnificent window displays for which the store was renowned.

Eventually, though, the old man cleared his throat and looked around the room, glancing at each of the board members in turn.

'I'd like to thank you all for being here,' Edward began, with a smile that Joss couldn't interpret. 'Especially at such short notice and on a Friday afternoon, when I'm sure you'd all rather be at a long working lunch. I'm afraid that, as some of you may have guessed, an emergency board meeting is rarely called to share good news, and today is no different. So, it is with regret that I have to announce that due to ill health I will be resigning from the company in all capacities with immediate effect.'

Joss felt fear and dread swell in an all too familiar

fashion in the base of his stomach as the deeper meaning of his father's words sank in. His father *must* be ill—seriously ill—to even consider leaving the business.

But Edward carried on speaking, leaving him no time to dwell.

'You all know that over the years we have taken steps to ensure a smooth transition when the time came for me to hand over the reins, and so—if you are all still in agreement—I will be leaving you in the capable hands of my son, Joss, who will become Managing Director and Chairman of the Board in my place. Eva, of course, will be assisting Joss in his new role, as I suspect she knows more about my job than I do. I know you will continue to support them, just as you have supported me. Now, I imagine there will be questions, so I'll answer them as best I can. Who's first?'

The room sank into silence as Edward finished speaking. Joss looked closely at his father. Ill-health? His father hadn't taken a day off sick in his life, and yet now he was resigning completely? Yes, they'd talked about succession plans. Any sensible businessman had contingencies for all eventualities, and Edward would not have wanted to leave the company in chaos if anything had happened to him. But had there actually been more to it than that? Had his father known that he would soon be stepping down?

The dread in Joss's stomach twisted into stark fear as the implications of the announcement sank in and he realised what this must mean. His father wouldn't resign because of a dodgy hip or 'a touch of angina', as he'd once described a health scare. He'd always sworn he'd be carried out of a Dawson's department store in his coffin. For him to resign must mean he had had some terrible news.

Panic and grief gripped his throat as he noticed for the first time the slight grey tinge to his father's skin, and the lines around his eyes that suggested a habitual wince of fatigue. Why hadn't he noticed before? Why hadn't he been looking? His father wasn't exactly a spring chicken, and he was still working sixteen-hour days long past the age when most people would expect to retire.

He should have made his father take things easier—should have taken more off his plate.

He met his father's eye and saw sympathy and understanding in his father's gaze. He wanted to rush to embrace him, but something froze him to his chair, chilling his blood.

And then warmth crept from the tips of his fingers as a hand slid into his and he heard Eva's voice.

'Edward, are you in pain? What can we do to help?'

Joss's eyes swam and he clenched his jaw, determined not to allow a single tear to fall, to keep control over his emotions. Besides, swiping a falling tear before anyone saw would mean taking his hand from Eva's, and at that moment he couldn't see how he was meant to do that.

'Perhaps we should speak in my office?' Edward said to Joss, his voice gentle. 'And you lot—' he addressed the remaining members of the board 'you have a good gossip while I'm gone and think of what you need to ask me. Head back to the pub and finish your lunch, if you want to. But get your questions to me sharpish, because I'm planning on being on a sun lounger by the end of next week.'

Edward rose and Joss noticed, as he hadn't before, that his father leaned heavily on the table for support.

Joss snapped out of his trance and back into business mode as they walked down the corridor and back to Edward's office, firing questions all the way.

'Dad? What's happening? Are you okay? Was this what you wanted to talk to me about?'

Edward collapsed into the chair behind his desk and rested back against the padded seat. 'Yes. I'm sorry, son. Of course I wanted to tell you first, but you didn't arrive for our meeting—'

'Dad, if I'd known—'

'I know.' He softened the words with a smile. 'I know. But it was difficult for Eva to get everyone here at such short notice. I couldn't delay it any longer.'

'Couldn't delay? What's wrong with you, Dad?'

'Sit down, son.' His father indicated the chair opposite. 'And you, Eva. You both need to hear this. It's cancer, I'm afraid, and there's nothing they can do about it. I ignored it for a bit too long, it seems. So I thought it was about time I took that holiday I've been promising myself for the last thirty years and let you get on with running the business while I'm still around to answer your questions—there's no deadline for you two, of course.'

Joss stared at his father, unable to take in his words. His hand found Eva's again and he gripped it hard, taking strength from the solid presence of her, the warmth that always radiated from her.

'How long, Dad?'

'Oh, you know doctors. Never give you a straight answer. A few months, it seems. Long enough to have a little fun before I go. I love this business—you know that I do—but news like this makes you rethink, and I don't want these four walls to be the last thing I see before I go.'

'I'm so sorry, Edward.'

Joss could hear the tears in Eva's voice, and he squeezed her hand. He knew how fond she was of his father, and that her grief must mirror his own. 'Are you sure you're comfortable? Is there anything we can do?'

'Quite comfortable for now, my dear. Thank you for your concern. Now it's my turn to ask the questions.' He glanced at their clasped hands. 'Is there anything you two would like to tell me?'

Eva sat in shock, silenced by Edward's words. She couldn't believe that the old man was dying. Sure, he'd looked a little creaky around the joints lately, but he'd never complained of so much as a runny nose. It just didn't make sense that he could be terminally ill.

Joss had taken hold of her hand and she could feel the contact burning her skin. She hadn't thought about it when she'd slid her fingers between his back in the boardroom. Hadn't thought about all the times she'd imagined the slide of his skin against hers over the years. All she'd been able to feel was the grief and fear radiating from him, and she had acted on instinct, trying to ease it in any way she could.

And now Edward was calling them on it. Under normal circumstances she'd have cleared up the understanding with Edward the minute it had happened. But this was Joss's father, and they had both just been hit with shocking news. It was Joss's place, not hers, to explain.

'I'm sorry you saw that, Dad—' he started.

'Oh, don't be sorry—I'm delighted. I *do* remember what it was like to be young, believe it or not. I'm just pleased that you two have finally found each other. I can't deny that I've been waiting for this for some time. I take it that if you're bringing your personal life with you to work then it's serious?'

Eva felt her mouth fall open and waited for Joss to correct his father, to sum up what had happened with the dress and the coffee and the zip. But expressions chased across Joss's face faster than she could read them.

She was just about to jump in and explain for herself what had happened when Joss finally spoke.

'Yes, it's serious,' Joss said. 'In fact, we're engaged.'

She was about to call him on being completely ridiculous when she clocked the look on Edward's face. A smile had brought a glow to his face, and he was beaming at them both. Just a moment she was so shocked she couldn't speak. And then real life kicked in, and she remembered the news that Edward had just delivered, that Joss had just received. She found that she couldn't contradict him.

Still, she gently withdrew her hand. She had to maintain some semblance of control if she was going to keep her head.

She'd been trying to pretend to herself for years that she didn't have an enormous crush on this man. That he didn't enter her mind when she was out on a date with any other guy. And now he had to go and pretend to be in love with her. And the only result of calling him on it would be to hurt the man she'd come to care for almost as a parent. She couldn't do it to him. She'd have to talk to Joss in private. He could break it to his father gently.

Funny how being angry with him made him that little bit less fanciable—she'd been looking for something to knock the shine off him for years.

It wasn't as if she *wanted* to be attracted to him— she told herself that often enough. She couldn't think of anyone less suitable for falling in love with than the son of her boss, who spent half his time on the road visiting the UK stores, and the other half in his office, buried in spreadsheets and dodging calls from disappointed would-be dates.

Secretaries talked—hardly breaking news.

As soon as she'd recognised where her feelings were going—the irritating pitter-patter of her heart, the annoying dampness of her palms, not to mention the completely inappropriate but delicious dreams that had her waking flushed and impressed by the breadth of her own imagination—she'd acted.

She'd put space between them at the office, avoided him in the break room and at the pub. She'd thrown herself into dating in a way that was the opposite of

Joss's clinical style: enthusiastically, prolifically, discriminately. She'd found handsome, eligible bachelors who weren't intimidated by her salary or her seven fluent languages—or the handful of conversational ones. She'd dated in Russian, Greek and German, and once—haltingly, but memorably—in Mandarin. She'd gone dancing, cocktail-making, picnicking. Tried blue blood and blue collar.

And not a single one of the men she'd kissed so demurely on the cheek at the end of the night had helped her even start forgetting about Joss. He was beginning to appear annoyingly unforgettable, and now he was pulling her into a deceit that she knew, unhesitatingly, was a BAD IDEA. All caps.

'Well, like I said, I can't say that I'm surprised. I've suspected for a while that you two have a soft spot for each other,' Edward said at last, still smiling.

Eva groaned inwardly. Oh, no, how much of her stupid crush had he seen? How much was he going to figure out? How much was *Joss* going to figure out for himself?

'And it makes me a very happy man to see you settled and in love before I go.'

The three of them sank into silence as the meaning of his words hit home and the reality of his illness intruded once again on the completely insane situation Joss had just created.

'But now I've got work to do—so get out of here, the pair of you.'

Eva kissed Edward on the cheek and mumbled something indiscernible, then let Joss follow her from the room, past the open-plan desks and into Joss's office.

'What the *hell* was that?' she demanded as soon as they were alone, staring at Joss as he sank into his chair and rested his face in his hands.

'Not now, Eva.'

'Not *now*? You just told your father we're engaged— I think I'm entitled to an explanation.'

'He's just told me he's dying. I can't talk about this now.'

She dropped into a chair opposite him, feeling sick to her stomach. Joss was right—he'd just had terrible news. Much as she had every right to give him hell, perhaps now wasn't the time.

'You didn't know anything about it?' she asked gently.

'He didn't say *anything*. Just that he needed to speak to me before the meeting. But I was tied up on a call and I… I missed the meeting. He wanted to tell me.'

'You couldn't have known he was going to tell you that.' She crossed to stand beside him and rested a hand on his shoulder. 'It wouldn't have changed anything. The news would have been the same.'

'It would have felt different if he'd been able to talk to me before having to tell everyone else.'

'You're right. I'm sorry.'

He leaned his head against her arm and she let her hand brush against his hair.

'And I'm sorry for what I told him about us.'

Eva moved her hand away, aware of a sudden change

of the chemistry in the room. She hitched herself onto the corner of the desk, letting her stilettoed feet dangle.

'What was that about? The truth would have been a much simpler explanation. It's going to be a hundred times harder to explain things now. Engaged or not, who knows what he thinks we were up to in his office?'

'I was thinking on my feet. I didn't want him to think that you were involved in something sordid, and my brain went to "engaged" rather than "wardrobe malfunction". You saw his face when I told him that we were getting married. I knew that it would make him happy.'

'Marrying me?'

'Being happy...settled. It's all he wants for me. And since my divorce... You don't want to hear all that. Just trust me on this one. I know my father. I knew it would make him happy.'

'So what's it going to do to him when you tell him there's no engagement?'

And suddenly, from the defiant clench of his jaw and the killer look in his eyes, Eva knew that he wasn't planning on telling his father the truth at all.

'Don't be ridiculous,' she said, keeping her voice low and commanding. 'We have to tell him the truth. I'll tell him about the coffee and the dress. I'll sort this out.'

Joss shrugged, never breaking eye contact, never backing down from the challenge she'd made so clear in her voice.

'We'll explain about the dress. But I see no reason to drop the pretence of our engagement.'

She stood slowly from the desk and took a step towards him, letting him know that she found neither his position in the company nor the six inches in height he had over her intimidating in the slightest. Least of all when he was seated and she could tower over him.

'No reason, Joss? You just panicked and told a bare-faced lie that has implications for us both. I have no intention of lying to your father, so unless you want him to hear from me that you just fabricated a fiancée, I think you would do better to just tell him now.'

'Or we could make him believe that it's true.'

She took half a step back to stare at Joss. 'Have you completely lost your mind? Why would we want to do that?'

'Maybe I have lost my mind. It wouldn't be the first time. I don't know... What I *do* know is that my father has just told me that he's dying, and I—we—can do something to make him happy in the time he has left.'

'By lying to him? Do you think he'd really want that?'

'You saw his face. You tell me if you think the lie hurt him.'

She shrugged, unable to contradict him. 'I know he seemed happy, Joss. But it can't be right. I mean, how long would we have to keep this up?'

She sat down again, losing a little of her anger as she realised what she was asking.

'I'm sorry. I didn't mean...'

'I know. I know you didn't mean anything by it. But, yeah, we would have to keep it up until he dies. Which, apparently, won't be all that long. Don't worry—I don't expect you to actually say *I do*.'

She sat and thought on it for a moment. Remembered the look on Edward's face when Joss had told his lie. She couldn't deny that he'd looked happy. As happy as she'd seen him for a long time.

She loved Edward. He had been the one constant in her life for so long now, and she wasn't sure how she was going to manage without him. A sob threatened, and her hand lifted slowly to her throat as she forced it down. She slumped into the back of the chair, suddenly deflated. Surely if it made Edward happy she could do this. She *should* do this.

'I need some time to think about it,' she said eventually, not wanting Joss to know the direction her thoughts had been heading.

Goodness knew she'd been trying to keep the details of her mind secret from him for long enough. If they were to go through with this completely ridiculous idea, how was she meant to keep that up? To hide the fact that her mouth wanted to part every time she saw him? That she had to stop her tongue moistening her lips and her body swaying towards him?

'Take some time, then. No work's going to get done this afternoon anyway, by the looks of it.'

Eva shook her head. 'Your father will need me.'

'I'm going to my father's office now, and we're going to have a long talk. I'll make sure there's not a problem. If you want, I can say you went home with a headache.'

'While he's still at work with a terminal illness? Thanks but no thanks. Lock yourself in with your father if you want, but I'll be at my desk if either of you need me.'

Joss leaned back in his chair, raising his hands to admit defeat. 'We need to talk, though. And we can't do that in the office. Dinner tonight?'

Dinner tonight.

How many times had she imagined Joss issuing an invitation like that? Though she'd always known that she wouldn't accept. It wasn't even the time that he spent travelling around the country that made her think he was a million miles from boyfriend material. No, it was the fact that even when he was here he wasn't quite...*here*. There was an isolation about him. A distance. Even when he was close enough to touch.

She'd done long-distance before, with people in her life that she'd loved, and she'd hated every second of it. The last thing she needed was a man—a fiancé—who was distant even when he was in the room.

But she couldn't ignore him while he was going around telling people that they had got engaged. She had to convince him to tell his father the truth. And then figure out how they were meant to work together.

'Yes,' she agreed eventually. 'I guess we do need to talk about this. My place? I don't feel like going out after news like this. I don't suppose you do either.'

'No. That sounds good. Eight?'

She nodded, and scribbled down her address.

Walking back to her desk, she grabbed the coffee-stained dress and put it in the garment bag that she'd flung over her chair as she'd raced for the boardroom.

The blinds in Edward's office were drawn—a sure sign that he didn't want to be disturbed—so she sat at her computer, knowing that her work—the one constant she had in her life—was going to change irrevocably, and there was nothing she could do about it.

CHAPTER TWO

EVA CHECKED ON the food and resisted glancing at her reflection in the window. She didn't want Joss to think that she'd made an effort, so she'd not touched her hair or her make-up since she'd got home, and had just thrown on jeans and a comfy jumper. She always wore her skinnies and a cashmere sweater for a Friday night in—that was perfectly plausible.

She didn't even want to think about how the conversation over dinner was going to go, but she had to. Had to be prepared—set out in her own mind, at least, what was and wasn't going to be on the cards.

Joss was crazy, thinking that they could get away with a fake engagement. They'd be under scrutiny every minute they were together at the office. She knew how little fuel the gossip furnace needed to keep it alight. But every time she convinced herself of how terrible an idea it was, she remembered the happiness on Edward's face and the eagerness to please his father on Joss's.

She had to admit to being intrigued.

Joss was a powerful man. A director—now the MD—of a vast luxury group of department stores, with a presence on every continent, property in every major European shopping capital. He was notorious for the coldness of his personal life—the wife and the marriage that he'd neglected, and the transactional nature of the dates he took to industry functions. The women he dated were always clients and colleagues, there to further a business deal or a conversation, and they always went home alone.

She'd always seen something else in him. Something more. Something in the way that he joked with his father in a way he didn't with anyone else. Being so close to Edward, she'd seen their father-son relationship up close. Seen that Joss might not be the cold-hearted divorcee that everyone had him pegged as.

And now he'd invented an engagement just to please his dying father, and her curiosity was piqued again.

The two men didn't have much time left together—and they both seemed happier with this alternative reality than with real life. Who was she to judge? Who was she to tell them they were wrong? If she hadn't been personally involved she'd be telling them to do whatever they had to do in order to enjoy the time they had left together. But to say that she was 'involved' was putting things mildly—and this was *way* personal. She'd be as responsible as Joss if the truth came out and Edward's heart was broken in his last few weeks or months.

And maybe all of this was academic. Because it assumed that they stood a chance of getting away with this charade. Making everyone believe that they were in love. Well, it wouldn't be too hard to convince on her side, she supposed, given the attraction that she'd been hiding for years.

Through the break-up of his marriage—that time of dark black circles under his eyes and an almost permanent blank expression on his face—she was the only one who had seen him lean back against his father's office door after he'd left a meeting, composing his features and erasing all emotion before he went and faced the rest of the office. And in the time since, he'd been working non-stop—not competing with his colleagues but seemingly competing with himself.

It was hard to pinpoint when she had realised she had a heck of a crush growing. Perhaps after the dip in her stomach when she'd won a hard-earned smile, or when they'd argued in the boardroom and he'd held up his hands in concession to her point, never mind that he was a director and she an assistant.

Or when he'd walked in on her today, half-dressed in his father's office, and her whole skin had hummed in awareness of him. She'd had to hide the blush that had crept over her cheeks when his fingertips had clasped the zip and pulled it down—something she'd fantasised about more times than she wanted to admit, even to herself.

But nothing that she had done so far had worked in trying to get herself to forget him.

Perhaps it was time to do something different. She had proved that ignoring this thing wasn't going to make it go away. Maybe getting closer to him was the key. It was easy to maintain a crush, a fantasy, from afar. When you didn't have to deal with wet towels on your bed or dirty dishes left on the table. Maybe what she needed was some old-fashioned exposure therapy.

Because what did she really know about Joss, beyond what she saw when he was occasionally in the office? If there was one sure way to test a romance it was for a couple to move in together.

Was she completely losing her mind thinking that this was even a feasible idea—never mind a good one?

The doorbell rang, shocking her out of her internal debate. Good, she was getting sick of the sound of her own thoughts. At least with Joss here she would have a sparring partner.

She jogged down the stairs to the street-level door, trying to ignore the familiar flip of her heart at the sight of him. Not that he was looking his best—he had clearly come straight from the office. His shirt was creased, his collar unfastened and his tie loosened.

And then she remembered again how his day had been a thousand times worse than hers and had to resist the urge to pull him close and comfort him.

'Hey—you found it okay?'

'Yeah.' He waved his phone vaguely at her. 'Just a little help from this. I've not been here since I was a kid.'

'Of course—your dad used to stay here back then. I'd forgotten you must have been here too.'

She stepped back so that he could get through the door. From her little cobbled mews she could barely hear the traffic from the main road nearby, muffled by the square of white stucco pillared houses around the private, locked garden. She showed Joss upstairs to her apartment—a legacy of the time when the building would have had stables downstairs and living quarters for servants of the wealthy above, all tucked away behind the grand mansions on the square.

Eva loved the understated elegance of her home, with clipped bay trees at the door, original cobbles paving the passage and soft heritage colours on the doors and windows.

'It's beautiful,' Joss said as he reached the top of the stairs and crossed to the living room, where great tall windows flooded light in one side of the room. 'Have you been living here long?'

'Since I started at Dawson's.'

Joss looked intrigued. 'I thought my dad had got rid of this place.'

'He had—sort of,' Eva said, reaching for a bottle of wine and raising a glass in question at Joss.

He nodded and reached to take it from her when it was full.

'He realised it was mostly sitting empty while it was a company flat, so he decided to rent it out. When I started working for the company I was stuck for somewhere to stay. Your dad didn't have a tenant at the time, and needed someone to house-sit, so he offered me this place.'

Joss raised his eyebrows. 'Lucky you.'

'Yeah, I don't like to move a lot, and he offered me a long-term lease. I like it here.'

'So I'm going to have a hard time convincing you to move in with me?'

Eva snorted, and winced at the sting of wine in her nose.

'That part's non-negotiable,' she confirmed. 'This is my home and I'm not leaving it.'

'So you're coming round to the rest of it? Good.'

She should have given him an outright no—told him there and then that there was absolutely no way she was going along with his ridiculous scheme. But somehow, with him here in her home, in her space, she wasn't sure she wanted to. All of a sudden she wasn't sure about anything.

That was what happened when the only stable part of your life upped and threatened to leave. It had sunk in on her short walk home from the office that she could be about to lose her job—the first point of stability she'd ever had in her life. The safe place that she'd built for herself in the twelve years that she'd been with the company.

She would have thought she'd have been used to it by now. She'd had her whole childhood to practise, after all. Every time her mother or her father had shipped out, or they'd all packed up and moved to another army base, she'd told herself it was the last time she'd care. The last time she'd cry.

She'd not managed to stick to her word until the final time. The time her mother hadn't come home at all.

Her father had packed her off to boarding school then, not long after she'd begged him to leave the army, to stop moving her around and give her some stability. She'd taken herself straight off to university after school, and from there straight into business, landing in Edward's team and working her way up to be his executive assistant.

Her parents had never managed to give her the stability she'd craved, so she'd found her own—with Dawson's. It was a family business, its history stretching into the last century and the one before that. The company had been around long before Edward, and she had no doubt that it would continue without him.

But how was it ever going to feel the same after he was gone? And what else was going to change?

The succession plans that had been approved by the board had appointed her as Joss's new EA—she was tied to the job role, not to the holder—but once his father was gone Joss had no reason to stick with that decision. She could be out through the door as soon as Edward was dead.

An engagement to the heir apparent—even a fake one—was another tie to the company. To the family. Another bond to the life that she'd built for herself. An obstacle between her and everything falling away. Was that completely crazy? Maybe. But that didn't mean she didn't feel it.

'Here.' She passed Joss a bowl of potatoes and a salad. 'Can you stick these on the table? The chicken will be just another minute.'

He took the bowls from her and glanced at the pan on the hob.

'That looks amazing. You shouldn't have gone to so much trouble, though. We could have ordered something.'

She shrugged. 'It was no trouble. I'd have been cooking for myself anyway.'

'You cook like this every night?'

She narrowed her eyes as she tried to work out his angle. 'Are you asking if that's part of the deal?'

'I'm making conversation. At least, I'm trying to.'

'I'm sorry.' She shook her head as she grabbed a couple of plates and started serving up. 'Everything just feels so…weird. I can't get my head around it.'

'It doesn't need to be weird.'

'Joss, this afternoon you asked me to pretend to be your fiancée. Now you're asking me to move in with you. How can it be anything *but* weird?'

'Because it's not real, Eva.'

She brandished a set of tongs at him. 'That makes it worse! How can faking something like that not feel weird to you? Lying to your father won't feel weird?'

He held his hands up and shrugged, though his expression belied his casual attitude. 'Do you tell your parents everything that's going on with you?'

'There's just my dad. We're not close. But I've never invented a fiancé.'

Before now, she added in her head. Because this conversation seemed to be gathering momentum, and she wasn't sure she was going to put a stop to it. She hadn't come out and told Edward that it wasn't true yet, so at the very least she was complicit in the lie getting this far.

It was only when Joss had mentioned it that she'd even thought about the fact that she might have to tell her dad. How was it that she'd put more emotional energy into worrying that she was lying to Edward than into the fact that she would also have to lie to her own father? She'd not even considered that going through with this would affect him too.

Maybe it didn't have to. Maybe she could keep the whole thing from him—it wasn't as if they spoke often. Or at all, really.

'You're quiet,' Joss commented as they sat down to eat at the dining table tucked into the corner of the living room.

'Thinking,' she replied, helping herself to salad and potatoes.

'Enlighten me,' Joss instructed, equally economical with his words.

Eva sighed, but he was here to talk and they weren't going to get anywhere if neither of them opened up. And, if what she'd seen of Joss over the years was anything to go by, she would be waiting a long time for an emotional outpouring from his end.

'I'm not sure that this is a good idea.' A good start, she thought. Get her cards on the table. 'We're lying to your father. It's likely we'll be found out. It's a distraction when we should be concentrating on what he needs.'

Joss raised an eyebrow.

'What?' Eva asked.

'We're doing it *for* my father. You saw how happy it's making him.'

Joss had said that they needed to talk, but it was only now she realised that he thought he was here to sort out details—not to convince her. He was assuming that she would just go along with it. He'd taken her decision not to tell Edward the truth from the start as approval, and he was here to iron out the fine print.

'You really think I'm going to go along with this?'

Joss looked up and held her gaze for a beat longer than was comfortable.

'I think you already are.'

A shiver ran through her at the tone of his voice. So commanding. So sure of himself. So arrogant. She'd had no idea before this moment that that did something for her, but the heat between her legs and the tightness in her belly told her it definitely did.

'If you were going to back out,' he continued, 'you would have done it back at the office. Or just told my father the truth on the spot. Why are we bothering to dance around this when we both know you've made up your mind?'

She fixed him with a stare and muttered an Arabic curse under her breath, trying not to show him how right she knew he was. Because she *could* have called a halt to this hours ago. The fact that she hadn't told them both all they needed to know.

'I'm doing it to make your father happy,' she clarified, still holding that gaze, making sure Joss could see that she wasn't backing down or giving in to him. She was making her own decisions for her own very good reasons.

'I know.' He nodded, taking a sip of his wine, breaking their eye contact and cutting into his chicken.

'I mean it,' he said, after he'd polished off half the plate. 'I could get used to this.'

'Good,' she said, standing up and picking up her

plate, suddenly losing her appetite. 'You can get used to doing the washing up as well.'

Joss finished his food and followed her through to the little kitchen. 'You think you're going to scare me away with threats of stacking the dishwasher?'

She gestured around the bijou kitchen. 'You see a dishwasher in here?'

He glanced around. 'Fine. So we'll get someone in. I'll pay,' he added when she started to shake her head.

'It's not about the money.'

'What? It's about me being willing to get my hands wet? Fine. But I'm not a martyr, Eva. If you're hoping to scare me then I might as well tell you now that it's not going to work.'

'You don't want to move in here. There's no space.'

He leaned back against the kitchen counter, a hand either side of his hips. His man-spreading made his intentions clear. It would have been more subtle if he'd marked the doorframe with his scent.

'I decide for myself what I do and don't want, Eva. This is where you live, so it's where I'll live too. You've stated your ground rules; now I'm stating mine.'

She folded her arms and leant back against the kitchen counter. 'There's not even any space in the wardrobe.'

'You can't expect us to live apart.'

'We're going to see each other all the time at work. Isn't moving in together a bit much?'

He took a step towards her, and Eva had to admit that his height *was* a little intimidating in the tiny kitchen.

'And how many people are going to believe our story if we're not living together?'

'We could tell people we're waiting until after the wedding.'

He shook his head and, much as she hated it, Eva knew he was right.

'They'd ask us which century we're living in. Perhaps if this was a real relationship we'd say to hell with what they think. But we need to make them believe us. I don't want to give them any reason not to. I'll start moving some stuff in on Monday.'

He moved to leave, and somehow, although it was what her rational brain wanted, it seemed her body wasn't expecting it. Disappointment washed through her. It wasn't as if she wasn't used to living alone. She loved having her own space. But they'd been through a lot today, and she wasn't particularly keen on being left alone with her thoughts.

'Do you want a coffee before you go?' she asked, flicking on the kettle behind her.

'Sure,' Joss said, watching her carefully. 'Something wrong?'

'No,' she replied, rubbing her forehead and realising she wasn't being very convincing. 'Just a lot to take in. Weird day.'

'Tell me about it,' Joss said, leaning back on the counter.

Eva looked up and realised that it wasn't a figure of speech.

'No, no—it's fine,' she said.

'I can listen. Even help.'

'I can't, Joss. He's your dad. You don't want to… It should be me asking if you're okay.'

'I don't get an exclusive on it, Eva. I know you care for him too.'

'I just can't believe I didn't know…you know.'

She made two coffees and carried them back through to the living room. Plonking them on the coffee table, she just had time to wish she had space for a bigger sofa before Joss appeared behind her.

'Do you sit and spy on your neighbours?' Joss asked, pointing out the way the sofa was angled towards the big picture window out onto the mews.

'More like bask in the sun. I get enough gossip at work.'

He looked surprised.

'What? Don't tell me you hadn't noticed.'

He shook his head. 'What do people gossip about?'

'Oh, you know—the usual. Who's sleeping with who. Who's angling for a promotion. Who's getting fired.'

'So why don't I hear any of this?'

Eva rolled her eyes. With all his expensive business education, did he seriously not understand how an office worked? She was clearly going to have to spell this out to him.

'Of course you don't hear the gossip,' she said. 'One, you're practically the boss. No one gossips in front of the boss. Two, you're hardly ever in the office. And three, you're not exactly Mr Friendly over the coffee machine when you *are* there.'

'People don't think I'm friendly?'

'*I* don't think you're friendly. I can't speak for anyone else.'

He folded his arms and fixed her with a stern look. She was tempted to laugh.

'What's so unfriendly about me?'

Should she go for it? Unload all his faults? All the reasons she'd been telling herself for years why he was a million miles from boyfriend material.

Why not? Perhaps it would be the final straw in this idiotic deception.

'Fine—if you want to hear it. You're not exactly an open book, are you, Joss? You don't talk to people unless it's directly about the business.'

'I don't do small talk. There's a difference.'

'Right: the difference between being friendly and not friendly. It's not a criticism. Just an observation.'

'You think I should be friendlier?'

She sighed and shook her head. Seriously, this man's emotional intelligence didn't even register on the scale. 'I didn't say that. I don't think you need to change. But just don't be surprised if people don't open up around you.'

'Well, *you* don't seem to be having a problem with that.'

She shrugged and gave a resigned laugh. 'Proposing to a girl will have that effect. If you didn't want to know, you shouldn't have asked.'

'Might as well know what people think of me. So— office gossip. Is there going to be a lot of it. About us?'

'Are you kidding?' She laughed properly, genuinely

amused for the first time all day. 'I'm going to be grilled like a fish about this on Monday morning.'

'You could just not go in,' Joss offered. 'Take a few days off. Benefits of dating the boss.'

The smile dropped from her face as the insult hit. As if she could just not show up for work, with no notice, and it wouldn't make a difference to anyone.

'I think we need to get a couple of things straight, Joss. One—I work very hard with your father. My job is important, and I can't just swan off because you say so. Unless you fancy handling his correspondence in Arabic, Italian and French on Monday morning, I'll be at my desk as usual. Two—we are not now, nor will we ever be "dating". If I'd wanted to date you, I'd have asked you out for dinner. I'm going along with your little charade because I care about your father. Don't confuse the two.'

'Would you?' He leaned into the arm of the sofa with a smile that was verging dangerously on smug.

'Would I what?'

'Have asked me out for dinner?'

She sighed. Bloody man. 'The key part of that sentence, Joss, was *if*. I've never asked you because I don't want to date you.'

'You know, you sound like you've given that quite a lot of thought. Should I be flattered?'

'Honestly. Only a man with your ego could find a way to take that as a compliment. Listen to me carefully, Joss. I don't want to date you. I don't want to be engaged to you. I'm going along with it for now. But when the time comes we'll both extract ourselves from this situation with as much dignity as we can muster and forget it ever happened.'

CHAPTER THREE

EVA SPENT THE weekend in a daze. The further she got from having seen Joss the more ridiculous the whole thing seemed. So when she pitched up at her desk at eight o'clock on Monday morning she was almost surprised to see him there waiting for her.

'You're in early,' she commented, unwinding her scarf from around her neck and draping it over the coatstand. 'Trying to impress somebody?'

'I told you—my father wants to start handing things over today. I thought we'd need an early start.'

'Well, we've both beaten the boss in.' She glanced through the blinds to Edward's darkened office beyond. 'Did you see him at the weekend? How is he?'

'*He* is marvellous, Eva, dear,' Edward said, bowling up behind her. 'Thank you for asking. And I was out of the city this weekend, so I've not seen anyone since I left the office on Friday. How about you two? I hope you did something nice with your weekend and didn't spend it worrying about me.'

'Dinner on Friday night,' Joss supplied truthfully.

'And Borough Market on Saturday,' Eva added.

No need to mention that she'd gone alone. She disliked the taste of the half-lie in her mouth, but the smile on Edward's face softened the blow.

'And arriving together on Monday morning. Were you this indiscreet before or am I really getting old?'

'Actually,' Joss said, 'we thought that now everyone will be finding out our news there's no reason we can't arrive together. In fact, I'll be moving my things over to Eva's place tonight.'

'Well, that's marvellous. Wish it had all worked like that when your mother and I were that age. Now, I'm glad I've found you two alone—I've been thinking, and there's something I want to say to you. I don't know what your plans are, but I don't want you to rush them for me. I know my news has been upsetting, but I don't want you hurrying anything up for my sake. Please?'

It was perfect, in a way, Eva realised. They wouldn't have to find an excuse not to marry before he died.

'But enough about that. I need the two of you in Milan as soon as you can get there. The store manager's feeling jumpy, and we have a couple of major suppliers over there as well who would probably appreciate a visit. I need you to smooth things over. Let people see that you're more than ready for the big job.'

Joss's eyebrows drew together, and she knew he wasn't happy at the implication that his employees didn't trust him.

'Dad, I met Matteo at the conference earlier in the year and it was all fine. The managers all know me. Surely you want me here? I'm not sure now's the time for me to be travelling.'

'Now's the perfect time, son. We need to steady things. You're going to have to visit all the flagship stores. The big suppliers too. They're worried—it's been a long time since this company faced big changes. This is part of your job now.'

'But what if something happens here?'

Eva winced. She knew exactly what Joss meant.

'What if I pop my clogs, you're asking? It's not going to happen overnight, son. We have some time. And I'd like to see the old girl looking straight before I go. I promise if anything changes you'll be the first to know. If it helps you make your mind up, I'm not planning on hanging around London waiting to die. Some places I want to see before I go. But you two need to be on a plane before lunchtime, and I've got an inbox the size of Milan Cathedral to work through with Eva before you go.

Joss walked away, leaving Eva and his father huddled around his computer monitor. Eva was making notes on a pad and occasionally reaching across to touch the screen. It was clear to him how fond she was of his father, and how distressed at the news of his illness.

And now he'd told them that he didn't want a hasty wedding. Yes, it got them out of having to take this charade too far, but Joss saw something else in it.

How much did his father know about his last marriage? About how he had felt rushed, unable to stop the oncoming commitment even after he'd realised it was a bad idea. More than he had let on at the time, it seemed.

He'd been rash and stupid announcing their nonexistent engagement to Edward, and he supposed that he should be grateful that Eva had agreed to go along with it.

She'd told him that it was because she cared for the old man, and Joss didn't doubt that. But that didn't mean he believed she'd given him the whole story. There were things that she was hiding. Layers of secrets, he suspected, from the frequently veiled expressions that crossed her face. Well, he was going to find out what they were—they had hours of travelling ahead of them, and she couldn't dodge his questions the whole way to Italy.

Or maybe he'd sleep instead of quizzing her, because that definitely hadn't been happening enough since his father had dropped his bombshell. He'd have liked to say it was grief over his father's illness that was causing his insomnia, but he knew that it was something else.

It was sleek chestnut hair and hazel eyes. The memory of a rose-pink slip under a serious navy dress. It was the thought of his holdall of clothes stashed in his office, destined for her flat just as soon as they got back from their trip. The thought of living in such close quarters with a woman he'd determinedly avoided since he'd noticed his attraction to her.

Back in his office, he dug out his toothbrush and a change of clothes from the holdall. If they weren't on a plane until lunchtime, he knew that they'd need to stay over. With his dad sending him off in such a hurry, he guessed it wasn't going to be a short meeting at the other end.

A noise caught his attention and he looked up to see

Eva, stalled at the entrance of his office. He felt that familiar pull, the heat in his body he knew was inevitable when he was near her. Again he silently cursed whatever impulse it was that had made him lie to his father.

He felt a twist of pain in his belly. He knew how dangerous secrets could be—keeping his feelings bottled up had turned toxic before, and lying to his father felt unnatural now.

Intellectually, he understood the reasons he'd done it. Because he'd let his father down so many times over the years. He'd married his university girlfriend, a friend of the family, because she was 'the right sort of girl' from 'the right sort of family', and everyone had expected it to happen. He'd done what he'd thought was the right thing—stood up in front of their friends and their family and made the commitment that was expected from him, no matter how wrong it had felt inside.

As his depression had grown and his marriage had darkened, he'd ignored the problems. Blinkered himself against his wife's pain and buried himself in his work rather than go back on his word and end a marriage that was never going to make either of them happy. Until she'd upped and left, and he'd seen the disappointment in his parents' eyes that he had failed. Failed his wife. Failed both their families.

It had only been after the breakdown of his marriage that he'd realised he needed help. He'd gone weeks with barely a couple of hours' sleep a night. Seen his weight drop and his appetite disappear. It had only been when he'd looked up his symptoms on the internet that he'd realised they were classic signs of depression.

As soon as he'd read that, everything had fallen into place—that was the dark tunnel that he'd found himself in as his personal life had hurtled towards marriage while he'd buried his head in the sand, concentrating on the business.

So he'd gone to his doctor, worked hard at therapy. Eaten and exercised well. Taken the meds he'd been prescribed. And he'd recovered from his illness with a clarity and a focus that he'd not felt in years.

He shouldn't have been in that relationship to start with. He should have called it off as soon as he'd had doubts—before his illness had blinkered his vision and left him feeling that he didn't have a way out.

His parents had hinted over the years since his divorce that he should start seeing someone else, get back out there. But he knew he didn't want to be a bad husband, a bad partner, again. He couldn't risk doing that to someone else.

But he also knew that his father wanted to see him settled and happy—that was what had made it so easy for those words to slip out of his lips in the heat of the moment. And it was what made him burn with guilt now, knowing that he was misleading him. He suspected his father felt partially responsible for Joss feeling he had to go along with family expectations. If this lie made Joss feel uncomfortable, it would be worth it if it meant that his father could let his guilt rest before he died.

The recent spate of sleepless nights was a worry, though. It was years since he'd felt this drag of fatigue, and it reminded him of a time in his life he had absolutely no wish to revisit. This time it carried with it an extra shade of dread. He didn't want to be ill again. Didn't want his world to shrink and pale as he fought with his own brain chemistry to feel even the smallest amount of hope.

And right there was another good reason not to listen to the pull of his body when Eva was near. No. They had to keep real life, real feelings, and their charade separate. Regardless of how attracted they were to each other.

He considered his own thoughts. Was he right? Was she attracted to him as he was to her?

'Hey, come in,' he said, remembering that she was still standing, watching him from the doorway.

She shut the door behind her and Joss shifted in his chair at the sudden charge in the room that their isolation created.

'How's Dad getting on?' Talking about his father seemed like the safest option.

'He's great. Same as always. If he hadn't told us, I still wouldn't know there was anything wrong. Says he's looking forward to some more time out of the city. You?'

'I'm good. Could do without this trip, if I'm being honest.'

'Yeah.' She glanced at her watch. 'That's what I wanted to talk to you about. Your dad's asked me to book us a room. Said he thought the meetings might go on a bit. I need to go home and pack a bag, so I'll just meet you at the airport.'

'It's easier if I come with,' Joss said, leaning back

in his chair. 'You're only around the corner. We'll get a cab from there. It means I can drop my stuff off too.'

'You brought it to the office?' Eva looked horrified.

'What? Are you still worried about the gossip?'

'It's easy for you to joke about it. You've not been grilled about our grand romance every time you've so much as looked at the coffee machine.'

'I'm sorry you're getting the brunt of it. Do you want me to say something?'

She sighed and shook her head. 'What? A formal announcement about our fake relationship? A little weird, Joss.'

'Fine. Well, we'll be out of here in an hour. Think the news has reached the Milan store already?'

'Oh, I can guarantee it'll travel faster than we do.'

As the plane lifted from the runway Joss itched to reach into his bag for his laptop, hoping to relax in the familiarity of a working journey. He'd travelled between stores more times than he could count, and he knew he could get plenty of work done before their meeting. Plus staring at the screen of his computer was safer than glancing across at the woman sitting beside him.

He remembered the first time he'd seen her. Well, the first time that he'd really noticed her. For so long during his marriage and his illness, he'd not been able to see any beauty in the world, never mind in a woman. And then one morning, newly divorced and with a fresh hold on his psychological wellbeing, he'd walked into his father's office and heard Eva speaking in quick-fire Italian—to the Milan store, perhaps. Or one of the luxury fashion suppliers. She'd burst into laughter, and as she'd thrown her head back in amusement she'd caught his eye.

Something had caught inside him, too. A spark of intense attraction he couldn't remember feeling since... Forget that. He'd *never* felt anything like that before—the intense pull not only to a beautiful woman, but to one he knew could joke and laugh in half a dozen languages when he was struggling to do it in one.

There had been a time in his past when an attraction like that would have felt like a red rag to a bull. But he knew better now. He knew where a relationship with him would leave a woman, and he had no desire to inflict that on Eva.

The 'Fasten Seatbelt' light was switched off, and Joss kept his eyes down as they both pulled out their laptops. Eva started muttering under her breath as she read through a document, the sound almost lost in the rustle of her hair as she tucked it behind her ear.

Please, not Italian, he pleaded silently. He wasn't sure what it was, but the sound of that language on her lips was his weak spot. He breathed a sigh of relief when he caught an Arabic phrase—something to do with the Dubai store, perhaps. It wasn't Italian but, *God*, she made it sound sexy.

He remembered the last time he'd heard her speak Arabic—at the conference of all their international store managers—the way the sounds had rolled around her tongue, and the confidence and speed with which she'd spoken. It was too much, eventually, and he glanced up from his spreadsheet, promising himself just a quick look at her expression.

But when he looked at her, her eyes were already focussed on him, and once he realised that he couldn't look away.

'What?' she asked him, breaking off from reading, and he knew he'd been staring too long.

He raised his eyebrows and shook his head. 'Nothing. Just wondered if you knew you were talking to yourself.'

He returned his gaze to the columns of numbers that had been dancing in front of his eyes since he'd loaded up the file.

He kept his eyes decisively on his screen until he heard his name pass Eva's lips and couldn't help glancing up to see her expression—he wished he hadn't when he saw the exasperation there. She rubbed her forehead and he glanced at her screen, but couldn't make out any of the Arabic she was reading. From her frustration, it was pretty clear that there was a problem, and he suspected he knew what it was.

'Trouble in Dubai?' he asked.

'They're worried,' Eva replied. 'Your father was due to have a phone conference with the manager of the store tomorrow. Edward's cancelled and asked me not to reschedule yet and the manager is worried about business continuity. I'm going to have to call your dad. See if he'll rearrange.'

'I'll take the meeting,' Joss said. 'What?' he added when Eva grimaced slightly.

'I'm not sure that'll work. In fact, I already tried that. They say they want to speak to Edward.'

'Well, if Dad's taking time off it's not like he doesn't have a good reason.'

'I know that. We'll talk to him about it when we're back in the office. But this is two stores just this morning who are going into crisis mode. I think we have to assume that others will react in the same way.'

Joss stared her down, not appreciating her doubting his ability to do his new job. 'I'm perfectly capable of running this business. I've been preparing for it for long enough.'

'I know that, Joss.' Eva relaxed back into the seat as she spoke. 'Your father does too—and every Dawson's employee, really. But knowing it and feeling it aren't necessarily the same thing. As a rule, people don't like change, and—like it or not—you at the head of the company *is* change.'

He shrugged off her concerns. 'So I'll go to Dubai too. To every single store worldwide if I have to.'

'It might help,' Eva said. 'In Dubai at least.'

Joss nodded, trying to mentally rearrange the next couple of weeks to accommodate another overseas trip. Dubai was too far to hop on a plane for just the day.

'You should come,' he said, thinking how valuable having his father's right-hand woman by his side would be in showing the store that nothing was going to change with him in charge. Yes, that was the only reason he was inviting her along. 'As a show of continuity. They might not know me well, but they know you. It will be reassuring.'

'I don't know, Joss.'

Eva didn't look convinced by his reasoning.

She leant forward, her elbows resting on the table in front of her. 'I never went with your dad. I can make the time to be out of the office for this one meeting, but I can't be constantly on the road or in the air.'

He watched her closely for a minute. The way she shifted in her seat and wouldn't meet his eyes. She might be worried about the business, but that wasn't really why she was refusing to go.

'That's not why you don't want to go. What is it—afraid of flying?'

She snorted a laugh. 'Did I miss you dragging me on here kicking and screaming? As if! And I'm an army brat, remember.'

'You *were* an army brat,' he corrected her. 'You look all grown up to me.'

He could have cringed at his cheesy line, but when her gaze finally locked on to his he didn't care—it was the truth. He didn't want to talk about her childhood. He wanted to talk about them on an all-night flight to Dubai and then getting hot and sweaty together in the desert.

He shook his head, hoping to scatter those dangerous thoughts. Eva was strictly off-limits, and he'd do well to remember that. Even if she agreed to this trip, as she'd agreed to the engagement, it would be strictly business. There would be no hot and sweaty—in the desert or anywhere else.

'So it's not the flight,' he said. He was intrigued. Who would turn down an impromptu trip to Dubai, with a visit to the city's most luxurious shopping mall guaranteed? 'What is it, then? Fear of catching some tropical disease?'

'It's nothing remotely exciting, Joss.' Eva flicked her fingers at an invisible piece of fluff. 'I prefer not to travel much. I love living in London and I like to stay there.'

Joss laughed with incredulity. 'But you speak six languages. Don't you ever want to use them?'

'Seven, actually. And, hello? How long have we been working together? I use them every day.'

'But is that really the same? Just saying the words, I mean. Or reading emails? Don't you want to go and experience the different cultures? Hear the dialects and the slang on the streets?'

Eva shrugged. 'I've done different cultures, thanks. I've done trying to learn what slang the cool kids are using. I'm happy where I am.'

'So why learn the languages at all?' He knew that talking about something so personal was probably a bad idea. But he couldn't help being intrigued by her. Couldn't help wanting to know more. 'There are plenty of jobs you could do without them.'

'It was a case of necessity at first, I guess,' Eva said. 'When we moved to Germany I wanted to do more than speak to the other kids on the base and at the army school. If I was going to be dragged to another country, I was determined to learn how to express myself there. The same when we went to Cyprus. And, to be honest, it came naturally. I loved learning to speak other languages. Maybe my brain likes the patterns of different grammar. Or hearing sounds that we don't even have in English. Words that can't be translated, because speaking another language makes you think in another language.'

'Okay, so German and Greek I get. But what about Arabic? Did you live in the Middle East?'

There was something more to this, he realised. Something about her parents. Something they'd never talked about before.

She shook her head. 'No, we were based here while Mum and Dad did their tours in Iraq. I'm not sure why I decided to learn. I quite liked the challenge of another new alphabet. A completely different written form of language.'

'And maybe it made you feel closer to your parents?' Joss asked gently. 'To speak the language they would be hearing around them every day?'

Eva remained silent, her eyebrows pulling together in a frown. Had she never considered that? he wondered.

'So, anyway, these meetings this afternoon,' Eva said, shaking off any suggestion of a personal conversation. 'What do you need from me? I've already requested an update from the supply management team on any issues they've had in the last few months, and pulled together the minutes from relevant meetings. As for the manager of the store, Matteo Lazzari, I've put all the correspondence between him and Edward in a folder and given you access. Is there anything else you need me to prepare?'

Joss looked at her closely, noting the swift change of subject but not pushing back. If she didn't want to talk about her personal life, then that was up to her. If this had been a real relationship then maybe he'd have encouraged her to open up, but this was just for show. She wanted to draw a line and that was fine by him.

He drew his eyes back to the spreadsheet in front of him, determined that the rest of the flight would be spent working, rather than trying and failing to guess what was going on in Eva's head.

When the announcement came to pack away all electronic devices and return their tables to an upright position, Joss congratulated himself on his self-control. Just as he'd promised himself, he'd got his work done with barely a thought for Eva.

He glanced sideways, to see if she was still working too, and realised the reason he had been so free from interruptions was because at some point, with her fingers still resting gently on her laptop keys, she had fallen asleep. Perhaps he wasn't the only one to have struggled with insomnia last night.

The cabin crew were making their way down the centre aisle, checking that their instructions for landing had been complied with, so he gently shifted Eva's hands from the computer onto her lap, then closed the laptop and folded up the table. She stirred a little in her sleep, shifting to get comfortable, and then eventually rested her head on his shoulder, letting out a deep sigh and settling back into sleep.

Joss watched her for a moment, unsure whether he should move her. But he thought it was unlikely he could do that again without waking her. So he left her where she was: with the gentle weight of her head against his arm and the smell of her hair temptingly close. The armrest between them was up, and as she fell deeper and deeper into sleep her body pressed closer, relaxing into him as he grew more and more tense.

He couldn't allow himself to enjoy this.

He mustn't allow himself to think about how he had seen that body covered only by the fine silk of a slip. How he'd wanted to run his hands inside her dress to clasp her waist, to pull her back against him as he slid her zip all the way down.

He couldn't allow himself to think about all the places his mind had taken him after he'd left her flat that night. Alone at home, he'd imagined pushing her dress off her shoulders, it gliding down to the floor and landing at his feet...

Another announcement from the cabin crew broke into his thoughts and was loud enough to wake Eva, who sat up with a start.

'Did I—?' Eva began, smoothing down her hair with a shaking hand before she stopped herself. 'Sorry—must have fallen asleep,' she said, briskly this time, looking around her in confusion. 'Did you put my laptop away?'

'They put the lights on for landing,' Joss offered by way of explanation.

'You should have woken me.'

He shrugged. 'Looked like you needed the sleep. I know the feeling. We'll be landing any minute,' he added, keen to move the conversation away from the question of them sleeping even in the same vicinity as one another.

An hour later their car passed the extravagant frontage of the Milan store on its way to their hotel, and he looked up at it in wonder. It didn't matter how many times he saw it, it never lost its magic. He thought of his great-grandfather, who had built up this business in a different century, a different world. And not for the first time he thought how lucky he was to be part of this family, to have such an inheritance, such a legacy to care for. His determination to continue that success, to prove himself, rallied.

And, much as he might protest to Eva that he had spent his life preparing for the top job, and much as that might be true, the job was his far sooner than any of them had imagined. He had thought he had a few more years to work on his relationships with the managers of the overseas stores. To build the connections that would be so important when his father was no longer around.

He was certain he had the experience and the expertise to continue the family success—now he had to prove himself to the rest of the business.

CHAPTER FOUR

Eva stepped up to the desk at the hotel and pulled out the paperwork with the details of their reservation. The receptionist took their reservation number and tapped the screen of the computer for a seemingly endless time, until eventually she looked up with a smile and called over a bellboy.

'Thanks so much,' Eva said, excited to be speaking Italian face to face, despite everything she had said to Joss on the plane. 'Could you send some lunch up to the room?' she asked as the bellboy took their bags.

Their meeting was in an hour, but with the prospect of Italian cuisine when they arrived she hadn't been able to face the thought of airline food.

'Something quick and simple, please.'

She hovered behind the bellboy as he jiggled the key card and opened the door into their room. As she followed him in, she realised that there must have been some sort of mistake, in spite of how long the receptionist had taken to check them in.

Her eye was first caught by the extravagant bouquet of flowers on the beautifully polished table in the centre of the suite's foyer. A bottle of champagne and a note sat beside it, with her and Joss's names picked out in a stylish copperplate hand. Through the open doors leading from the foyer she could see at least one bedroom, a marble-lined bathroom, and a terrace overlooking the city. It was luxury far beyond anything she'd ever experienced. Was this what she had to look forward to as part of the Dawson family?

Not that she was part of the family yet. *Or ever would be*, she reminded herself. This engagement was all for show, no matter how real this suite was making it feel.

She picked up the envelope and turned it over, feeling the heavy weight of the paper in her hand. She read the note inside, fighting against the tear that was threatening at the corner of her eye.

Dearest Joss and Eva,
Consider the suite a little engagement present
from me. Enjoy Milan and don't hurry back.
Love,
Dad

Those last two words made her feel something she had been looking for for as long as she could remember. Included. Accepted. Part of a family. Something her own family had never managed.

Some parts of her childhood had been so privileged she knew she shouldn't complain. She'd always had a roof over her head and food on the table. While her mother and father had taken turns to be away on tour, among families and homes torn apart by conflict, whoever had been left behind had tried their best to fill the space that was left.

But that didn't change the facts. Both her parents had been happy to leave her for months at a time. Hugging her goodbye and promising to be home soon, all the while aware that they had no way of knowing if they could keep their promises. And then—inevitably, it had seemed—her mother had kissed her goodbye, told her she would be home soon, and instead they'd had a visit from a sombre-looking man in uniform. Eva had been left with the knowledge that her mother had never loved her enough to want to spare her the pain that her death would bring, even though she'd tried to convince herself that she didn't care enough to hurt.

She'd thought that would be it for her father. That he would be repulsed by the thought of leaving her again. Of taking the chance of making her an orphan.

She'd been wrong.

Joss came up behind her and took the note gently from her hand.

'The old romantic,' he said, with the beginnings of a laugh. He stepped around her to examine the champagne, but when he caught sight of her face he replaced the bottle in the ice bucket and reached to touch her cheek. 'What is it?' he asked, alarm evident in his expression.

'It's nothing,' Eva said, painting on a fake smile. 'You're right—it is romantic. Shame it'll be wasted on us.'

A knock at the door signalled lunch arriving.

'You show them in, I'll be back in just a minute.'

In the bathroom, she patted cold water on her cheekbones and took a few deep breaths, trying not to think about romance, or the suite, or Joss. It was probably a good job that they were going to be in meetings all the time they were out here. It didn't matter what Edward said—she would be hurrying home. The less time they spent closeted in a luxury hotel suite the better. Or safer, at least. There were a lot of reasons why she might enjoy being locked away with Joss, but it was absolutely not a good idea to think about them. Definitely safer not to.

She left the bathroom and grabbed a couple of pieces of ciabatta from the tray the waiter had left on the table. Eating while she worked, she sifted through the files that she had brought with her, stocking her bag and ensuring that her tablet had enough charge to last the rest of the day. She had access to all the information that Joss might need for their meetings. This was his first test as Managing Director of the company, and it was a matter of professional pride for her that nothing went wrong for him.

She glanced at her watch as she pulled on a jacket. 'Are you ready?' she called to Joss, who had disappeared into one of the bedrooms.

'Be right out,' he called back.

She checked her phone as she waited by the door and was relieved to see a text from their driver, letting them know that he was waiting for them outside.

Joss emerged wearing a fresh shirt and she deliberately averted her eyes, not wanting to give herself any excuse to appreciate the way that man wore simple white cotton. It was a thought that she'd blocked out a lot over the years—when she'd caught sight of Joss in a meeting or walking through the office and tried to work out exactly what it was that made this man so attractive to her.

It wasn't as if he was even *nice*. Sure, he was courteous. He was professional. She couldn't think of a time when he had been outright rude. But definitely not nice. He wouldn't go out of his way to make someone feel comfortable. Wouldn't remember her birthday and drop something small and wrapped on her desk in the morning without a word.

He was nothing like his father, whom she adored. So how was it that for years she hadn't been able to get him out of her head? Why was he the man she measured every date against and found them lacking?

She reached behind her and grabbed the door handle, opening the door into the corridor and stepping out of the suite when Joss was a few feet away. A buffer zone: that was what was needed. Safe space between them that couldn't be breached.

But would people think that was odd? she wondered. She had no doubt that news of their engagement would have reached the Italian store before they did. Her standoffishness might cause more gossip—make people start to question whether the relationship was real. Make them ask what she hoped to get out of it.

She shook her head. It was far more likely that people would see that they were two professionals at work, acting professionally. No one would expect them to be all over each other. Respectful distance worked *for* their story, rather than against it.

'So, when was the last time you met with Matteo in person?' she asked Joss, determined to keep their conversation on a work footing after their earlier diversion into her personal life.

'In the spring,' Joss said. 'But it was at the conference for all the international store managers. You know what that thing is like—between meetings and presentations there's hardly time for a business conversation, never mind anything more personal.'

'Well, we should have lots of time today. You two have all afternoon pencilled in, and there's nothing in your diary for tonight either, so you can always take it to dinner if you feel you need to. Just remember you're trying to make a personal connection. He knows that you're capable. You've been with the company for ever. Just show him that you're someone he's going to enjoy working with.'

Joss caught up with her in the hallway. 'What? You want me to flirt with him? Seduce him?'

Here she was, trying to be professional, and he had to mention flirting and seduction pretty much the minute he opened his mouth. Was he determined to make this impossible for her?

'You know, I think he's been happily married for the last twenty years or so. I'm not sure flirting will get you anywhere.'

Joss tutted. 'You know what I mean. You think I should charm him. That's what he wants?'

'I don't think he wants to be charmed, Joss. I think he wants to get to know you. You could be friendly. That would be a start.'

Friendly. There was that word again. Was that what she wanted from him? For him to be friendly to her? Hardly. That would make things impossible. At least when he was terse and short and—well, *un*friendly— she could remind herself of all the reasons why she shouldn't indulge this crush of hers. If he were to actually start conversing, or—God forbid—laughing like a normal human being, then she was going to be in big trouble.

'I thought we'd already established that I can't do friendly.'

'No, we established that you *don't* do friendly. Only you know whether that's out of choice or not. Do you try to be unfriendly?'

'I just try and get the job done, Eva. It doesn't normally require chatting over a cup of tea.'

'Well, your new job does, Joss. People need to see you, to get to know you. Your dad's illness has been a big shock to everyone. They're going to miss him enormously. It's a big gap to fill.'

Joss stopped in the hallway and fixed her with a stare.

'I'm well aware of that, thank you, Eva.'

She let out a breath and reached out a hand to his arm. 'I'm sorry, Joss. I know you are. And I'm not trying to criticise. Just trying to fill you in on what your father's relationship with his store managers is like. I'm not saying that you need to do business in the same way—I'm just giving you the information that you need to manage this transition. We're all trying to manage this situation as best we can. Myself included.'

He turned back to the lift and pressed the button to take them to the lobby. 'Well, thank you for the information. I'll take it under advisement.'

So that was how today was going to be. Icy cool. Well, that was fine by her, but she wasn't sure what Matteo would make of it.

They walked into the grand entrance of the Milan store to see Matteo waiting to greet them. 'Eva, *bella*. It is always such a pleasure.' He greeted her with a kiss on each cheek and warm enquiries about her health. 'And Mr Dawson, of course.'

He held out a hand to Joss and received a brusque handshake in return.

'Please, call me Joss.'

Unfortunately Joss's tone didn't match the friendliness of his sentiment, but Eva resisted the urge to roll her eyes in front of Matteo.

'And I hear from a little voice back in the office that congratulations are in order! You are to be married?' He kissed Eva again on both cheeks and shook Joss's hand again. 'An office romance. How lovely.'

He picked up Eva's left hand and let out a murmur of dismay.

'Oh, but no ring?'

'Oh, no,' Eva said, trying to think on her feet. 'Everything happened rather quickly, and with Edward's news…'

She let the sentence sit in the air and hoped that her allusion to terminal illness would do away with the need for further explanations.

'Oh, but you have some time now,' Matteo exclaimed with pleasure. 'And you are in the most beautiful store in the world! If you will forgive the slight to your English stores, Mr Dawson. I absolutely insist you come and choose something before our meeting.'

Eva looked at Joss, expecting him to shut down any discussion of shopping and insist they all get to work. But he wore an inscrutable expression that was heading towards a smile, and somehow she knew that meant trouble.

'If you're sure you don't mind waiting a little longer for our meeting, Signor Lazzari. Eva and I would love to do that.'

As they walked through the lobby towards the fine jewellery department, Eva grabbed Joss's hand and hung back a little, allowing the distance between them and Matteo to stretch beyond his hearing a whisper.

'What are you doing?' she asked out of the side of her mouth, glancing round to make sure that no one else could be listening in.

'Being friendly,' Joss replied with that same almost-smile.

'If you're doing this to make a point to me, it's fine. I get it—you're Mr Friendly. Time to drop it.'

Joss shook his head. 'Matteo wants to spoil us in his store. Show it off at its best. I thought it was politic to go along with him. Anyway, we will need a ring. If we wait too long people will start to talk.'

'You know,' she said, a touch of sharpness in her voice, 'some people think of that before they pop the question.'

'Yes, well, I'm not "some people", am I? I have the feeling that you never would have agreed to this if I was.'

She stopped, a hand on his arm turning him towards her. 'And what's that meant to mean?'

'Oh, nothing, darling,' Joss replied as he realised they had reached the gleaming glass counters of the jewellery department and Matteo was looking at them expectantly. 'So—where do you want to start?' he asked.

Matteo pulled out a few rings from the nearest cabinet—diamond solitaires all of them, ranging from the shockingly big to the tastelessly huge.

'Something classic, perhaps?' Matteo said, handing her a platinum diamond ring that must be a good three carats.

Eva held it between her fingertips and then looked up to Joss. He must have sensed her discomfort, because he took the ring from her and placed it back in the tray.

'Something a little more unusual for Eva, I think,' he said, reaching for an equally huge stone, this time flanked with pretty yellow pear-shaped diamonds. 'What about this,' he asked, meeting her eyes as he slipped the ring onto her finger.

She stood staring at it for a moment, reality and make-believe clashing. She knew this wasn't real. She knew it was all for show. But with this rock on her finger the lines were less clear than ever before.

She couldn't deny that she'd fantasised about this moment. All she wanted in her life was constancy... stability. Perhaps, one day she'd meet a man who she wouldn't want to let go. He'd slide a ring onto the third finger of her left hand and she would know without doubt that it was staying there for life.

It wasn't meant to feel like...*this*. It was never meant to be temporary. All she could see when she looked at this ring was the day when she would have to take it off. When Edward was gone, and she and Joss gave up their pretence, she'd have to return it to its snug velvet box and hand it back to him.

Her eyes filled with tears, but she fought them back, knowing that she couldn't lose it in front of Joss, never mind in front of Matteo.

'Ah, look at you. This is a special moment,' Matteo said with a smile. 'And I see I am not quite needed here. If I say I will see you again in an hour, will that be enough time for you?'

He handed Joss the keys to the jewellery cabinets and clapped him on the shoulder. 'I leave you two young lovers alone. Choose something special, yes?'

They both watched in silence as Matteo crossed the jewellery hall, waiting until they were alone and could speak safely.

'You don't like it?' Joss asked eventually, picking up her hand again and examining the ring.

'It's spectacular,' Eva replied with honesty.

'Then why the tears?' he said, gently this time, brushing a finger across her cheekbones.

'I'm not crying.'

'You're not letting them fall. I can see that. But you're upset. Why?'

'It's nothing, Joss. It's just that this is all a bit unnecessary. It feels strange. Wrong.'

'Why?'

There was no impatience in his voice, nor in his expression, as she took her time choosing the right words.

'Because it's all a lie. And a ring like this—it deserves something better. It's meant to be a symbol of love and commitment. We both know that we're not promising either of those things.'

He looked down at the ring for a moment, and then gently pulled it over her knuckle. 'Nothing that looks like an engagement ring, then. That narrows our options. What about this?' he asked.

'That's an eternity ring, Joss. Same problem.'

'You know, I don't think the ring is going to mind.'

She shook her head, not sure if she could make him understand without revealing too much of herself. '*I* mind. I might want one of these things for real one day. When I buy my engagement ring—or an eternity ring for that matter—I don't want to be keeping the receipt for when I have to return it.'

'So that's the problem.' Joss nodded, looking as if he had cracked a particularly difficult problem in the budget spreadsheet. 'You don't want something you like because you won't want to give it back? You can keep the ring, Eva. With everything you're doing for my father, for the business, it's the least I can do.'

Eva let out a breath in frustration. 'It's not about the money, Joss. It's the symbol. It's what the ring's meant to mean. I can't accept an engagement ring when there is no engagement.'

He looked thoughtful, and remained silent for a few long minutes, before reaching for her hand and pulling her gently to another case. 'What about if the ring symbolises something else, then? What if it's a gesture—a friendly gesture—of thanks. Thanks for caring for my father enough to go through with this. Thanks for looking after him and the business for so long. It's a gift—from a friend. The meaning doesn't change, whatever happens between us. And I absolutely won't accept it back from you when this ends.'

She looked at the case of jewellery he had brought her to, and thought about what he had said.

A gift like that she could accept, she thought. A ring was part of making this engagement look realistic, but these didn't look like engagement rings. They looked more like garlands of flowers, or boughs of blossoms. Tiny diamonds, sparkling and weaving their way across bands of yellow gold.

Joss unlocked the case and brought out one of the rings, with pink and blue sapphires scattered amongst bigger diamonds. He slipped it on to her third finger and they both stared at it in silence for a moment, taking in the effect.

'What do you think?' Joss asked.

'Better,' Eva said. 'It feels…friendly.'

Joss breathed a laugh. 'You old romantic. You're right. It's better. But it's not perfect. It's too heavy for those slender fingers. Too busy.'

He slipped it off again, and swapped it for a more delicate one—just diamonds this time, set in a meandering line like a trailing spray of flowers. This time when Joss slipped it on her finger she had no doubts.

'It's the one,' she said, gazing down at her finger.

'Perfect,' Joss agreed.

And before she realised what he was doing he had lifted her hand to his mouth and the warm heat of his lips was pressing against her knuckles.

She stood and stared at him, not quite sure where to begin with her line of questioning on this one.

'Joss… I don't think…'

His lips left her hand and he looked up, meeting her eyes with his intense gaze. She forgot what she had been going to say. Something about how this wasn't a good idea, probably. Except with her hand still encased in his, with the ring warming on her finger, it suddenly felt like the best idea they'd had for a while.

Joss's other hand landed lightly on her waist and for a moment neither of them breathed. Then, as one, they took in a sharp breath, and nudged closer towards one another.

Joss's hand snaked around her back, taking hers with it, twisting her until her back was against the jewellery cabinet. And it would have been so, so easy to relax into him, to loosen her body and let his arms take her weight. Take her anywhere he wanted to go.

Another half-step closer and his body met hers, pressing lightly against her from knee to chest, setting off fireworks everywhere in between.

This was all for show, she reminded herself. Joss was playing a part. For him, all this was just a way of making his father happy. Nothing about this was real for Joss—not in the way that the feelings she could feel growing for him were real.

At that moment she heard Matteo's voice from somewhere behind Joss and pushed gently against his chest, putting some much needed distance between them.

'Ah, I see you two have chosen something. Come—let me see.'

Eva held her left hand out to Matteo, hoping that she would be able to control the slight shake she could feel deep inside.

'It is beautiful,' Matteo said. 'A wonderful choice. But then I would expect nothing else. So, perhaps now we are ready to get to work?'

'Of course,' Joss said, his voice brusque, nothing like the soft tones she had heard when they were discussing her engagement ring.

She hoped that Matteo would put it down to an excess of emotion over their engagement rather than unfriendliness, otherwise the whole 'choosing the ring' exercise would have been wasted.

'And I have just spoken to Signora Lazzari—Giulietta—and she insists that you join us for dinner tonight,' Matteo said.

'Oh, I'm not sure if we—' Eva started.

'We'd love to,' Joss said, interrupting Eva's plan for a polite refusal.

But Joss was probably right. He was here to show the manager that he was the sort of man they could work with. It made sense for them to have dinner together. Eva herself had suggested that they might spend some time together this evening. But eating together as a foursome—that was inviting a world of trouble.

When they were working, it would be simple to explain away the lack of intimacy between them. They *should* keep a professional distance when they were in the office or one of the stores. But at dinner, perhaps at Matteo's home, that would be personal. They would be expected to look like a couple—and they'd have to make it convincing.

But now that Joss had agreed she didn't have much choice. She could hardly *un*accept a generous invitation from the man they were here to charm.

'But I insist that you allow us to take you out,' Joss said, allaying one of her concerns.

At least if they were safely out in public then they would be expected not to indulge in too many displays of affection.

CHAPTER FIVE

Eva PULLED ON the black dress that she always packed in case of emergencies. There was no situation she'd discovered yet that a simple black shift couldn't handle. She caught sight of the diamonds on her left hand and decided to leave off the statement necklace she'd also packed—it would be a shame to overshadow the pretty, understated ring that she and Joss had chosen together.

They'd agreed on dinner in the hotel restaurant downstairs. Its reputation was unparalleled in the city, and Matteo and his wife had happily accepted Joss's suggestion.

She checked her reflection quickly in the mirror and rubbed away a smudge of eyeliner. She'd kept her make-up simple, professional: a subtle reminder to herself that she hadn't knocked off for the day. She still had a part to play.

She heard the shower being shut off in the other bathroom and wondered whether Joss had thought to pack something to wear out to dinner. If it had been Edward taking the meeting she would have provided him with an itinerary of their trip—including likely social possibilities as well as all the meetings that were confirmed in the calendar. She hadn't found that familiarity with Joss yet. That closeness. A way of anticipating his needs even before he did.

She shivered slightly at the thought of developing such a thing with Joss. Even without their fake engagement, the changes at work would have been enough to turn their relationship completely on its head. To break down those careful barriers she'd built to keep herself distant from him at work. To keep her mind from wandering in his direction.

With everything else that had happened, she hadn't stopped to consider the alternative reality that might have existed if Edward had never walked in on them in the office and got the wrong idea. It wasn't as if her life would have carried on unchanged. She and Joss would still be in Milan, for a start. In separate rooms, though, instead of this suite. And Joss would still be moving in to Edward's office, sitting every day in her direct eyeline, on the other end of an intercom, occupying a huge part of her work life.

Joss's presence in her life would have grown anyway. So maybe by agreeing to this engagement she'd actually gained more control than she would otherwise have had. More freedom to discuss the nature of their relationship. To make clear to him that, however it might seem, a romantic attachment was absolutely *not* on the cards between them and never would be.

She shook her head. Most people didn't feel the need to have that sort of conversation with their boss. With most people it was just assumed that there would be nothing extracurricular going on. Just the fact that she was thinking it proved that these changes were always going to have caused trouble.

'Are you ready?' Joss called from the other side of the bedroom door.

What a question. She was ready to jump in a car, get on the first plane home, and pretend that none of this was happening. But was she ready to go out and fake a relationship with the man she'd been burying her feelings for since his divorce? She wasn't sure she wanted to admit the answer to that one.

Instead she opened the door, shut out her feelings and faked a smile.

'Ready,' she said, doing a last-minute check on the contents of her bag as they headed to the front door of the suite.

'You look nice,' Joss said as they headed out into the corridor.

He'd barely looked at her, she noticed. But she couldn't fault his manners.

'You too,' she replied, trying just as hard not actually to look at him.

Spending so much time together was meant to be curing her of her crush—but so far all the evidence was that it was having the opposite effect. It really was in no way fair. Perhaps it was the vast suite that Edward had arranged for them. With their separate bedrooms the size of palaces they might as well be living in separate apartments, as they had been back in London.

But this was only temporary, she reminded herself. Tomorrow they would be flying back to London, where there was a holdall of his clothes waiting for them in her spare room. And an empty drawer and a few inches of wardrobe space she'd managed to clear out for him.

They rode the lift down to the lobby in silence, and Eva deliberately avoided meeting Joss's eye in the mirrors that surrounded them. Then she remembered what they were doing here, the lie they were meant to be living, and risked a glance at him. She found him already watching her, and gave him a small smile.

'Ready for this?' he asked.

'No. You?'

'No.'

At that she felt the smile spread from her lips and across her cheeks, and saw it was reflected in Joss's eyes. She even risked a small laugh.

'Well, as long as we're in agreement, I suppose.'

She grabbed his hand as the lift doors slid open, and they were greeted by the sight of Matteo and his wife waiting for them in the lobby. Good job they'd got their faces sorted out before the lift stopped, Eva thought.

She greeted Matteo and Giulietta with kisses to both cheeks, but Joss kept her hand locked in his. She held on, in case he needed the support. Anyway, with her body anchored to his like this it made it easier to remember what she was doing—the part she was supposed to be playing. She wasn't just his assistant, greasing the wheels of conversation, providing snippets of information when they were needed. She was half of a couple.

Even as they were chatting over an aperitif she could still feel the warmth of Joss's hand against her skin, and she wondered if that would ever go. This hyper-awareness of his body whenever it was in contact with hers. In twenty years, would she still be getting fireworks if their fingers brushed when she handed him a letter to sign, or a contract to approve?

Twenty years.

Working with Edward, she'd never had any trouble envisaging her future. She'd felt secure. She'd known—or thought she had known—that she would always have a place with Dawson's. But now… Now she couldn't be sure.

One of the reasons she'd agreed to this charade in the first place was because she'd thought it would bind her more closely to the company, and then Joss wouldn't be able to show her the door as soon as his dad was gone. But was that naïve? Did this fake relationship make it more likely, rather than less, that Joss would want to see the back of her once this was over? Surely it would be more realistic that they *wouldn't* want to work together any more if they 'broke up'.

And if people found out that the whole thing was a sham, of course Joss would want her out of the way.

The thoughts crashing through her brain made her realise how naïve they had been, thinking that they could just start this thing with no idea when or how it was going to end. And how had she thought that Joss would want to keep her around after it was over?

A shiver ran through her, and she felt rather than saw Joss turn towards her.

'Cold?' he asked, dropping her hand and placing an arm around her shoulder.

'Just from this,' Eva said, faking a laugh and gesturing to the Prosecco in her hand, condensation beading on the glass.

As they took their seats at the table Eva was still incredibly aware of her body language, and that of Joss, sitting beside her. Were they playing it too cool? This was a dinner with colleagues, and they were out in public, so no one would expect them to be all over each other. But since she'd shaken off Joss's arm, with protestations that she wasn't cold, she was more aware than ever of his presence beside her, of having him so close but not touching.

Should she do something? she wondered, as she stared at the menu in front of her, unable to take in a single word. She glanced at his hand, resting on the table, and wondered if she should reach for it. She could just slide her fingers between his, the way she remembered doing instinctively the day Edward had announced his illness. It would look like the most natural thing in the world to Matteo and his wife. Or maybe she could rest a hand on his thigh, feel under her fingertips those firm muscles which just a couple of hours ago had pressed her against a jewellery cabinet.

She resisted the urge to sigh and tried to concentrate on her menu instead, picking it up from the table and attempting to focus.

'Oh, what a pretty ring,' Giulietta said from across the table. 'Matteo told me you chose it together today.'

Eva smiled at Giulietta and glanced down at her hand. She remembered what Joss had said about it symbolising friendship, her place in the family, and looked up at him with a smile.

'Ah, but you two are so in love,' Giulietta said with a laugh, and Eva felt her cheeks colour. 'It is good that you can be happy after such sad news. I was so sorry to hear that Edward is not well.'

This time she didn't think about it. She reached for Joss's hand and squeezed it tightly in her own, knowing how raw his pain must be, if it was anything like her own.

'Thank you,' Joss said, carefully steady.

Eva glanced up at him and could see from the set line of his jaw how much of a struggle he was finding that composure.

'I know my father values your efforts here highly.'

'And I know that he is so sorry that he's not able to be here himself,' Eva added, hoping that she'd be able to make up for Joss's lack of warmth.

Edward and Matteo had been friends for years, and she knew that the Lazzaris would be feeling the sadness of his loss too. Joss had his own grief to deal with—but she had to make sure that this meeting achieved everything they needed it to. Matteo *had* to see that he would be happy working with Joss.

'I know that he would love to be at this dinner with us.'

'Ah, we understand,' Giulietta said with a kind smile. 'We are just happy to have *your* company this evening. And to be able to send our warmest wishes with you when you return.'

'Of course we will take them,' Eva said, and glanced up at Joss.

They were here to try and show Matteo a more

human, personal side of Joss, but so far he was too distracted. He seemed more buttoned up than ever, and she still had no idea how to get him to open up.

'If you'll excuse me?' Giulietta said, pushing her chair back. 'I'll be back in a few moments.'

Three at the table felt a whole lot more uncomfortable than four, Eva realised after a few seconds' awkward silence.

She attempted to start up a conversation a couple of times, but nothing was thawing between them. Matteo's phone rang, and he excused himself from the table with apologies, saying that it was his deputy at the store.

'What?' Joss asked, as she turned towards him with a concerned look.

She took a bracing breath, knowing that this conversation had to be quick, discreet and effective. 'We're here to show Matteo a warmer side to you, yes? Well, we're not doing a good job so far.'

He sat up a little straighter in his chair. 'We were talking about my terminally ill father. Would you like me to be cracking jokes?'

She shook her head—a small, efficient movement. 'Of course not. And I understand how difficult it will be. But we've come all this way. If we're not going to make it count, then why did we bother? Do you want to go back to the office having failed to achieve our objective?'

She knew that the business-speak would win him over—she'd worked with him for long enough to understand that the company director in him wouldn't be able to resist the threat of a missed objective or deadline.

Giulietta returned to the table and Eva greeted her with a smile, and an offer to top up her glass. Signora Lazzari took hold of her hand and looked again at her ring.

'Forgive me,' she said. 'I can't help looking. They're pretty stones—and such an unusual design. You really have an eye.'

It was the perfect opening she needed—cue Joss's human side.

'Actually, it was Joss's choice. He understood exactly what I would want.' She turned to him with what she hoped would look to their guests like an adoring smile.

'After a couple of false starts,' Joss added with a laugh.

Eva could hear that it was slightly forced, but from the look on Giulietta's face she hadn't noticed.

'Let's just say that Eva had to point out the virtues of "less is more".'

Joss leaned over and pressed a kiss to her temple, and for that second when his lips were on her skin everything else stopped. The noise of the restaurant... the conversation around the table. Her breathing and her heartbeat. Everything was *him*. His lips, his touch, his heat.

And then it was gone, and the world crashed in again—noisy and brash.

'Well, you must be an attentive pupil,' Giulietta said. 'It's truly beautiful. And have you set a date?' she asked as Matteo returned to the table, tucking his phone into the inside pocket of his jacket.

'It is to be soon?' Matteo asked as he took his seat. 'Your father must be so excited to see you married.'

'We don't want to wait longer than we have to,' Joss said, taking Eva's hand. 'But we're not ready to set a date yet. My father has asked us not to decide anything until we've had time to come to terms with his news and all the changes it will bring. He wants us to concentrate on business at the moment. We feel that's the least we can do for him, to ensure the continuation of his legacy.'

'Ah, well, a long engagement is very romantic,' Giulietta said with a sigh. 'Sometimes I wish we could go back and do it all again.' She looked wistfully at her husband. 'Be newlyweds again.'

'I can drink to that,' Joss said with a smile that looked a little more relaxed. He lifted his glass. 'To engagements.'

'And being a newlywed,' Giulietta added.

Matteo lifted his glass as they all toasted.

'And to Edward Dawson,' Matteo said before they all went to replace their drinks on the table. 'He can never be replaced, but I am looking forward very much to getting to know his son better.'

Eva breathed a sigh of relief, and for the first time since they had arrived in Milan thought that maybe this might turn out not to be the disaster she had feared.

The rest of the dinner passed quickly, with conversation flowing in tandem with the wine. They eventually kissed Matteo and Giulietta goodbye in the lobby, late in the evening, and walked towards the lift, still hand in hand, just in case the Lazzaris should look back and see them.

Except Eva didn't drop Joss's hand once they were in the lift. She felt warm and comfortable, relaxed in Joss's company in a way she hadn't been since the day Edward had shared the news of his illness and Joss had come up with his absurd plan.

Until the lift doors slid shut and they were completely alone.

Not so relaxed any more.

In fact every muscle in her body tensed as she glanced around her, seeing them reflected in the mirrors on every side of them. Still their hands were linked together. She looked up at Joss, to find that he was already staring down at her, his expression inscrutable.

She opened her mouth to speak, but the ding of the lift stopping and the doors opening halted her.

Hand in hand, they turned towards their suite, and Joss dipped his free hand in his pocket for the key card, smoothly opening the door so that they barely had to break stride.

Eva realised she was holding her breath. She wasn't sure when she'd started to do it, but as the door closed behind them, and they were truly private for the first time all evening, she let it out—long and slow. All she could think about was Joss's lips. Warm on her hand that afternoon as he sealed their friendship ring with a kiss. And then tender on her temple over dinner.

She stopped at the door, not trusting herself to go any further into the suite. After all, her hand was still locked in Joss's, and neither of them was showing any sign of letting go.

She leant back against the door and Joss stood in

front of her, filling her vision with the wide shoulders of his exquisitely cut suit.

'Everything okay?' he asked, his voice low and sensual.

Eva nodded, when what she really wanted to do was shout. To tell him that no, she wasn't okay. That things were far, far from okay. This was confusing and terrifying and oh, so much more complicated than she had ever wanted her life to be.

But she couldn't let go of his hand. Couldn't be the one to break that connection between them.

She'd felt it growing as they'd played their parts over dinner. A touch of the hand here. A brush of fingers over an arm there. A quick kiss to the temple and too many shared smiles.

The intimacy had grown and grown between them, in some strange simulacrum of the relationship they had invented. But she had expected them to walk away from it. Expected to leave it at the table as they had their dirty glasses and used tableware. She hadn't expected it to stalk them into the lift and back up to their suite.

Intimacy was safe in public, where neither of them could act on it. But with her back against this door and Joss in front of her—looking serious, smelling delicious—it was a more dangerous prospect. And Joss knew it too. That much was clear from his expression. And she wouldn't be the first person in her family to walk headfirst and knowingly into danger. Maybe she had more in common with her parents than she'd realised.

A shiver went through her as the moment to push

him away, to break their contact, came and went, and she knew that she had made a decision. She closed her eyes and pushed herself onto her tiptoes, then gently, as gently as he'd kissed her, she pressed her lips to his.

For a moment she thought she'd miscalculated, misjudged, and that this *hadn't* been where the evening had been heading since the moment she'd walked out of her bedroom and set eyes on Joss. But then his lips came alive beneath hers, tasting, touching, caressing. She let out a long sigh—her body's relief after so many years of imagining this moment.

But her body wasn't the one in charge here—her brain was, and it wasn't exactly cheering her on. She could feel his restraint, too. It was there in his jaw, when she touched it gently with her fingers. It was there when he lifted his hand and it came to rest on the door beside her head instead of on her cheek or in her hair. It was there in the way he held his body ever so slightly away from hers, instead of pressing her hard into the wood.

And it was there in the way she had her hand on his chest, making sure he couldn't get too close.

She broke the kiss and rested her head back against the door, a chagrined look on her face.

'Bad idea,' she said at last as their breathing returned to normal. 'Too complicated.'

'I wish it wasn't,' Joss replied, and she could tell that he meant it.

Except they'd known each other for years before it had got so complicated, and they had known then, too, that this wasn't a good idea. At least it was a kind lie.

'Goodnight,' Eva said at last, after a few long moments during which one or the other of them might have decided that the complications didn't matter that much after all. But this wasn't a fairy tale, and the realities of their lives weren't going to melt away because of one kiss.

She pushed herself away from the door, determinedly avoiding eye contact, and brushed her hand gently against his arm as she slipped past him and into her bedroom.

CHAPTER SIX

'*BAD IDEA,*' EVA had said. Joss couldn't argue with that. It would undoubtedly have been a very bad idea. But a bad idea had never looked so good in his life.

They could have just gone for it. One kiss—how much damage could that have caused? But instead they'd both held back, and the whole moment had turned into a glimpse of what it might have been. Stirring his imagination without satisfying anything.

The next morning that kiss was on his mind all through his meetings with the Milan-based suppliers, even as he was reassuring them that there was no reason to think that there would be any drop in demand for their luxury goods throughout the Dawson's network of stores. And there would be absolutely no problems with the transition from Edward's leadership to his.

And on the plane, with Eva so close and so untouchable, the impression of her lips on his remained distractingly present.

It wasn't until they walked into their office at three o'clock in the afternoon and saw his father packing the contents of his desk into cardboard boxes that he was able to push that kiss from the forefront of his mind.

'What are you doing?' Joss barked at his father as he reached his office, though the answer was startlingly obvious.

'Sorry, son,' Edward said. 'I thought I'd be finished before you were back from the airport. You're the boss now—it's only right that you have the office that goes with it.'

Joss folded his arms, looking around the messy office, unable to believe his father was really going to be gone. 'Dad, I don't need your office. I don't *want* your office.'

'Well, I don't have much use for it now, and it would be silly for it to sit here empty.' Edward held up his hands and shrugged. 'And, really, I'd quite like to see you sitting here. If it makes you feel any better, it means Eva won't have to move desks. You'll want her close, believe me. She knows this job as well as I do. Better.'

He'd want her close. Well, there was the problem, wasn't it? It seemed that neither of them knew exactly how close they wanted to be.

She'd kissed him yesterday, all the while keeping him at a safe distance, never really giving in to what she wanted, even when they were alone. And he'd held back too. Warring with himself, telling himself that he had to stop this. He'd not been able to drag his lips from hers. All he'd been able to do was keep some emotional distance and try as hard as he could not to be dragged by those sensations into doing something they would both regret.

He whipped his head around as he heard the familiar click of her heels behind him.

'Edward—no. You can't be packing up already.'

'Ah, my dear, you as well. It is good to see you and my son so in tune with one another but, really, you must both see that I'm not needed here any more. Joss is more than capable of running this company and, to be perfectly honest, I've got places I would rather be. You know how much this business means to me—both of you do. But a prognosis like mine helps you to see what's really important. I've given this business fifty good years. Now, if I only have a few months left, I'm going to spend them doing some of the things I've been putting off for too long.'

He taped up the box with what seemed to Joss to be an unnecessarily dramatic flourish.

'Now...' He glanced at his watch. 'I've got an appointment, so I guess the rest of this will have to wait until tomorrow.' He laid a hand on Joss's shoulder as he passed him. 'I know this is hard, son. I'm here if you need to talk.'

He left the office and Joss couldn't breathe. It was as if he'd taken all the oxygen with him. He sat stiffly against the edge of the desk, among the abandoned staplers and office supplies that Edward had left lying there.

'Do you?' Eva asked.

Joss stared at her, unable to work out what she meant.

'Do you need to talk? Because I'm here too.'

He absolutely, definitely did not want to talk. What he wanted was to go and lock himself in his own office and get on with his job as if none of this was happening. There was a budget spreadsheet in his inbox that he could happily lose himself in for hours.

But he'd been down that route before, and it hadn't led anywhere good. Anywhere healthy. He had no intention of going there again. Talking to Eva… He wasn't sure that was a good idea. But when he thought about it he wasn't sure there was any other good option. She was the only one who knew the secret they were keeping after all. But what about *his* secrets? What about all the things in his past that he'd carefully hidden from everyone around him.

'Maybe I *should* talk, Eva. But I'm not sure that talking to you is the best idea. After last night…'

'What about last night?'

Really? Was she just going to pretend that it had never happened? Maybe they both should. After all, forgetting about that kiss was just about the most sensible—albeit impossible—option at this point.

'That kiss. It was…nice.'

He had a feeling it might have been incredible—if they hadn't both been holding back. He didn't know what her reasons were, but he was going to have to share his if that was what it took to keep them both from the mistake of making this fake relationship real. She had to see what a bad idea it would be, getting involved in a relationship now, with his father's illness and the knowledge that they would lose him soon.

'But I think we were right to stop it when we did. Taking it any further… It just wouldn't be a good idea.'

'Oh!' Eva's left hand flew to her chest. 'You mean

this isn't for *real*?' She subtly waved her engagement ring at him, but the rolling eyes gave her away. 'I *do* know that, Joss. Really, you need to get over yourself.'

'I know I wasn't the only one holding back, Eva. And I don't need you to tell me your reasons. But I want you to hear mine. It's not like I didn't want—'

He stopped himself before he said something stupid.

He started again. 'I want you to understand why. You know that I've been married before?'

Eva nodded.

'Well, it didn't end well. For either of us. The thing is, before I got married I was ill. But I didn't realise.'

She looked curious at that, but didn't interrupt.

'It was clinical depression. I hid it from everyone. From my family. From my then girlfriend, now ex-wife. I didn't get the help I needed, and then the wedding gathered pace around me, and I found myself in the position of being a really terrible husband.'

Her eyes softened with sympathy. 'But you were ill, Joss. It wasn't your fault. Maybe you need to be kinder to yourself.'

He stood stiffly, determined that she would understand him. 'I know that depression is an illness, but that didn't make our marriage any easier for my wife. Or our divorce, for that matter. I realised after it was all over how wrong it had been to feel the way I had for a long time and I finally got help. Got better. But none of that changes what I put her through. Or the fact that I know that it could come back. I'll never be completely free from it. And I'm determined not to do to anyone else what I did to my ex.'

Eva took a step closer to him and he took half a step back. 'You don't know that you will get ill again,' she said.

'And I don't know that I won't. What I *do* know right now is that my dad is dying, and that seems as good a recipe for depression as any other I can think of.'

'And don't I get a say in this?'

He looked at her closely. Had he missed something? This had started as a way of getting things off his chest, just to make things clear to her. A way to avoid the bottling up of his thoughts that he knew could lead somewhere toxic. She had been holding back too last night, and he'd assumed that meant that she was as wary of this chemistry between them as he was. But was he wrong? Did she want more?

Her answer unsettled him—he'd never really thought that she'd want a say in it.

'Don't look at me like that,' she said. He hadn't realised he was looking at her like *anything*. 'I'm not saying that we were wrong to stop things.'

He walked away from the desk and she shifted herself up to perch on the edge of it. He couldn't tear his eyes away from her ankles, slender and vulnerable-looking atop her smart spike heels.

'Look,' she continued. 'I think we can both say that there is an attraction between us. After what happened last night it would be stupid to attempt to deny it. But I'm as scared of this thing as you are. No offence—and this has nothing to do with what you've just told me—but a relationship with you would scare the hell out of me. I want commitment and stability, and even before I knew what you just told me it was abundantly clear that those things are not of interest to you. I fancy you—okay. But that doesn't mean that wanting you is a good idea. We got carried away last night. It was the first time that we really had to act this thing out, and it was trickier than I expected to slip in and out of character. We'll get better at it. We have to.'

She fancied him? It shouldn't really be news to him—not after that kiss last night. But somehow, despite everything else she was saying, that was all he could hear. And not because it was a nice boost to his ego. But because it made him question so many things from the last few years. All those times he'd avoided her, knowing that she was too much temptation, had she felt the same?

'But just because I don't think this would be a good idea, Joss...' she slipped off the desk and came towards him, laying a gentle hand on his arm, '... I don't think having an illness in your past is a good enough reason to shut yourself off from the idea of having a relationship in the future. There's probably some woman out there who thinks you'll make the perfect boyfriend— and she should probably be allowed a say in what happens. Why don't you give it a chance?'

He thought for a long moment. Some mystery woman who might come and convince him that he had been wrong about the decisions he had made in his life? He just couldn't see that happening. If he couldn't find it in himself to bend his rules for Eva, he just couldn't imagine any other woman who would make him want to.

'Well, we don't need to worry about that, do we?'

he said briskly, wanting out of this conversation before he started questioning his own better judgement. 'For now, I'm an engaged man. And one relationship—even a fake one—is enough.'

'Fine.' Eva said, crossing her arms. But then her expression and her body language softened. 'But I meant what I said. If you want to talk, Joss, or if you think your depression might be coming back...you can come to me. I mean, a fake fiancée can still be a pretty good listener.'

Joss smiled. If things had been different—if he hadn't had this illness lingering in his past—he was pretty sure she'd made a damn good *real* fiancée.

'I appreciate that. So, what about you? No luck finding a stable, committed guy to do this for real?'

'Plenty of candidates,' Eva said, with a shrug that wasn't as nonchalant as he thought she was hoping for. 'None that quite match up to my criteria.'

'Lucky for me, I guess.'

'Damned lucky for you.'

CHAPTER SEVEN

EVA SAT AT her desk, watching the clock on her screen ticking ever closer to seven o'clock. It was already dark outside and the office had emptied a couple of hours ago—everyone except her and Joss were long gone.

She wondered whether Joss was working late for the same reason she was—putting off the moment when they would have to go back to her little apartment and start living together for real. Her stomach gave a growl, and she wished she had picked up something more substantial for lunch.

Well, one of them was going to have to be the first to make a move, and she was too hungry to wait and see if Joss would cave. She shut down her computer and straightened up her files for the morning.

Joss appeared in the doorway to his office, leaning against the frame.

'Heading home?' he asked.

'Yeah, I'm all done for the day. And starving,' she added truthfully. 'I'll see you back there.'

She opened the door to her flat and headed straight for the kitchen. She hadn't shared her living space since she had left university and started working at Dawson's, and she realised that she had no idea how adult flatmates really worked. Or any form of cohabiting other than student living, really. She'd not seen her parents living together often enough to have formed an idea of it at an early age. How *did* a relationship work with both parties present at least most of the time?

She hated feeling so uncertain in her own home. For as long as she had been working at Dawson's she'd felt settled, secure. She'd known how things worked in the office; she'd had her own place to come home to. No one had started changing things up just when she'd got settled. And now her security at the office had gone, and even her home wasn't the safe haven it was meant to be with Joss moving in.

She chucked the leftover sauce she'd found in the freezer into the microwave and tested the pasta. Still way too *al dente*. A glance out of the window showed no one coming up the mews, and she felt relieved. Perhaps she'd be able to eat and zone out in front of a box set for an hour before Joss came home. At which point she could invent some excuse and escape to her bedroom for the rest of the evening.

Really, Eva, she chastised herself. *Hiding? Not exactly your style.*

But then the glow of a mobile phone outside the window caught her eye and she knew that her plans for a solo dinner had just been thwarted.

When she heard the knock at the door she remembered that Joss didn't have a key—something they'd have to fix. As she walked down the stairs it really hit her. He was going to be here. Every day. Even if not in person, his stuff would be here. He was going to be a permanent presence in her life for the next few months at least.

She tried to think of the last time she'd had a relationship, even a friendship like that, and came up blank. The last man she'd lived with was her father. And that hadn't exactly been plain sailing.

She opened the door and stood aside to let Joss pass her on the stairs, but instead he stopped in the doorway and gave her a considering look.

'What's wrong?'

'Nothing,' she replied automatically, trying to shake off the mood that thinking about her parents always caused. 'Just thinking that we need to get you a key cut. Come up—I've put some pasta on.'

'I thought you told me not to get used to being cooked for?'

'You shouldn't. You're cooking next time.'

'Fine. It's a date. I told you—you're not going to scare me off with threats of domesticity.'

A date. She hadn't meant it to sound like that, but intentionally or not she'd just arranged one. Did Joss see it like that too? Or was it just a figure of speech?

She shook her head as she went back up to the kitchen and gave the sauce a stir. Of course he didn't see it like that. He couldn't have been clearer with her that he didn't want to date her. Good, because she'd already told him—more than once, and in no uncertain terms—that she didn't want to date him either.

And where did that leave her? she wondered, thinking back over the last few years of her love-life—or lack of one. If she didn't want to date the only man she had been remotely interested in in years, then was she resigning herself to a lifetime of being alone?

Maybe there wasn't anything wrong with that. Lots of people never married. Stayed single. Perhaps that was the life she was cut out for. When this engagement was over Joss would move out, she would move a couple of cats in, and settle for the next few decades.

But if she really thought that why had she bothered dating at all? Why download the apps and accept the blind dates and chat to the hopeful-looking men in bars if she wasn't looking for something more?

Window shopping—that was what she had been doing. After their visit to the Italian store's jewellery department yesterday, she recognised it for what it was. Looking at all the pretty things on offer, knowing they weren't right for her, and that she would never be interested in actually buying them. So why wasn't she interested in dating Joss either? If the only reason she hadn't wanted those other guys was because they weren't *him*, surely she should want him if he were offered on a plate.

But it wasn't just about him, she realised. Maybe it had never been about him. If she refused to accept anyone who wasn't Joss, but didn't want the real thing either, then that left her where? On the shelf? Off the market? It left her alone, as she had been for all of her life. Where she was comfortable.

Was that what this was?

'Hey, is it terrible to open a bottle of wine on a Tuesday night?' Joss asked, grabbing one from the rack beneath the kitchen counter.

'After we spent most of Monday night on the Prosecco? I don't think anyone will judge us too harshly.'

She was glad of the distraction as she opened the bottle and found glasses.

'So, what have you got planned for the rest of the week?' she asked, trying to keep their conversation on a safe work footing as they went through to the living room and settled with bowls of pasta on their knees and their wine on the coffee table.

'Ah, I actually need to talk to you about that.'

'Sounds ominous.'

She'd expected him to brush the comment off, but he nodded. *Not good.*

'It's Dad. He's invited us to spend the weekend with him. He wanted an engagement party, inviting the great and the good. I managed to talk him out of it, but he still wants us to spend some quality time together.'

'Just the three of us?'

It was a lovely idea, in theory. She couldn't think of a better way for Joss and his father to spend the time they had left. And she loved Edward—of course she wanted to spend time with him. But this charade of a relationship with Joss made everything more complicated. By spending time together, were they going to expose their secret and do more harm than good?

After what had happened in Milan she knew that spending more time in close quarters with Joss and an audience wasn't a sensible idea. Acting out their relationship with the Lazzaris had led to acting out her desires, and they had both agreed that that had been a bad idea. The last thing they needed was a whole weekend of blurring the boundaries.

But they had to put Edward first. And if it was a weekend of quality time that he wanted, then that was what he deserved.

'Yeah, just the three of us,' Joss replied. 'Unless you want half the county and your business contacts list invited too?'

She shuddered. She wasn't sure what was worse—the scrutiny of the single person who knew them both better than just about anyone, or of everyone either of them had ever met.

'The whole weekend?' she checked, thinking that maybe, if they went for just a few hours over lunch, they might be able to keep up the pretence without doing too much harm to her self-control. Being together a whole weekend, there was no way that they'd be able to get away with separate bedrooms—not when Edward thought they were living together.

'That's what he said. And, given the circumstances, I want to go. It's not like we have time to waste.'

'And he wants me there too? Are you sure?'

Joss nodded. 'Of course he does. He thinks you're my fiancée. He just assumed that you would be coming. And you have to admit it would look strange if you didn't.'

Of course it would.

'Okay. And it's just one night, isn't it? Two at most?'

Joss nodded. 'We'll drive down after work on Friday. Be back on Sunday.'

She drew her brows together in confusion. Edward's house was no more than a fifteen-minute walk from her mews, on one of the smart garden squares that filled this part of London.

'Drive there? Wait—where are we going?'

'The house in Berkshire. I thought you realised that's what I meant?'

She sat back in the sofa cushions, temporarily lost for words at the thought of being isolated down a country lane with Joss. Somehow the seclusion of a country house seemed more intimate than being in London all together. If they were in the city she could make excuses to give Joss and Edward time alone together—pop out and fetch them all coffee, suggest a trip to the gallery she knew was opening on Saturday. In the countryside she didn't even know if there would be a pub nearby to escape to if it all went wrong.

She shook her head, but knew that she couldn't refuse. 'Of course I'll come—it'd be my pleasure.'

Oh, she shouldn't have used that word. Because now all she could think of was all the different types of pleasure that Joss could show her in an isolated country house. Hot breath on cold cheeks after a walk to a secluded spot in the woods... Cold hands on warm skin in front of a roaring fire...

'And the rest of the week?' she asked, knowing that she needed to distract Joss from what she was sure was a tell-tale blush on her cheeks.

'Dubai,' he said, giving her a curious look. 'You were right. I need to show my face. Let them know everything's going smoothly. Make sure everyone's happy with how things are going to work from now on.'

She nodded. 'Sounds like a good idea.'

'I need you to let me know if there are any problems here,' he went on. 'Make sure the place is running okay with Dad not coming in to the office any more.'

'I'm your eyes and ears on the ground. I get it. Do you want me to book your tickets?'

'It's done,' Joss said.

Eva felt piqued that he had bypassed her.

'What?' he asked, when he saw the look on her face.

'I know all this fiancée stuff is pretend, but you *do* know that the job isn't? I'm your assistant. I should know about your travel plans.'

'You're angry that I got someone else to book my plane ticket?'

'I'm angry that you're not letting me do my job. The other thing doesn't trump that, you know. I know it's hard, with everything else that's going on, but we have to find a way to work together as well. Otherwise how will that look? Like you've taken over and I'm instantly getting an easy ride.'

'Well, at least one of us is…' Joss said.

Eva didn't want to begin to unpick all the potential meanings of that sentence. Way too dangerous.

'Fine,' he said. 'While I'm away you can take over everything that's needed. When I'm back you can brief me on anything you think I need to know about from my father's desk that he hasn't already covered. Does that meet with your approval?'

'Fine. Good.'

She knew she still sounded short with him as she took another sip of wine, but she prided herself on her professional skills. If Joss was going to work around her at every opportunity she couldn't see herself *wanting* to stay in her job for much longer—a thought that terrified her. If she didn't want to be at Dawson's any more she didn't know who she was, never mind what she wanted from life.

No, she was being silly. Her job at Dawson's went way beyond her relationship with Joss, and mattered way more. She wouldn't even consider leaving just because she and Joss hadn't worked out the finer details of their professional relationship yet.

'So, when do you leave for Dubai?' she asked, wondering when she would get back the safety and security of living alone.

'I thought I'd go Tuesday, then be back in time to drive us down on Friday. Does that work with my diary?'

'You'll have to tell me. Until we get to work tomorrow I'm officially off the clock,' she said, taking a glug of her wine to prove her point.

CHAPTER EIGHT

EVA GLANCED AT the time, hating herself for doing it even as her eyes were drawn once again to the hands on the old wooden grandfather clock in the far corner of Joss's new office.

Three forty-seven. Exactly four minutes after she had last looked.

And at least twenty minutes after she had expected to see Joss back in the office.

He had been on a half-nine flight, which the live arrivals board told her had arrived at Heathrow at thirteen thirty-three. If he'd jumped into the car that she had booked for him he should definitely be here by now.

It was professional concern, she told herself. He had a meeting at four o'clock. She'd told him he would be cutting it fine if they were to leave to pick up his father this evening and get to the house, but he'd insisted that he would be there in time.

Her eagerness to see him was nothing to do with the way she had lain in bed awake, remembering the hard press of his body and the gentle touch of his lips in that hotel suite in Milan. Thinking about the night they had spent together in her flat, knowing that he was just down the hall. Knowing she could bump into him on the way to the bathroom and get a glimpse of those firm, toned abs and muscular thighs.

She shook off the thought. No, it was absolutely nothing to do with that at all.

A noise behind her made her jump, and she turned to see Joss striding through the office, familiar holdall in hand, glancing at his watch.

'I know, I know—you told me it would be close.'

'And you told me you'd make it. I never doubted you,' she lied.

He came up to her desk and kissed her on the cheek, and it was only as the blush rose that she remembered he was only doing what would be expected from a man who'd just spent a few nights away from his fiancée. He was performing for their audience, who—a brief glance out of the corner of her eye told her—were appreciative of his efforts.

'I told him you'd meet him in his office,' she said after a pregnant pause, suddenly struck with stage fright, unsure of her lines.

'Great. I'll drop this bag and head over there now. We'll still be out of here by six. Promise.'

She smiled and waited for him to walk away, but his gaze hadn't broken from hers and the ghost of a smile passed over his lips.

'Did you miss me?' he asked.

She resisted the urge to draw in a shocked breath, keeping her breathing deliberately slow and even. Was he playing with her? Was this part of their act or was he really asking her—the *real* her, not the fake fiancée?

'Not even a tiny bit,' she said, with a proper smile of her own.

Any eager ears in the office could put that down to normal relationship banter, she decided. And it was worth it to see the expression on Joss's face. She liked taking him by surprise.

He reached out a hand to her cheek, just ghosting the tips of his fingers along the line of her jaw. 'Well, I guess that means I need to make more of an impression,' he said, his voice low. Too low to be for the benefit of their audience. 'Give you something to miss next time I'm gone.'

He brought his right hand up in a mirror of his left, bracketing her with his fingers. She should pull away. Turn her face to her computer monitor in an effort at professionalism. But then she might never know. She would be left wondering whether this was for play or for real. And suddenly, dangerous or not, she had to know.

For the fleeting half-second he held her gaze, she wondered if she would be able to tell. And then she remembered that kiss in Milan. The way that they'd read everything the other person was feeling through the touch of their skin. And she knew that his body wouldn't lie to her, whatever he might say out loud.

With the first fleeting, barely there caress of his lips, she knew that it was real. It held all the promise of their kiss in Milan. Set off all the same fireworks. She lifted her hand to his face, felt the same tension in his jaw— the strength of his desire battling with the strength of his self-control. She could feel herself teetering on the edge, just as she had in Italy, knowing that letting a crack in her resolve show for even a second would mean they were both lost.

Which was why—even as it pained her—she pulled away. Again. Put just a millimetre of space between them, waited for him to move further back. He didn't. Instead he leaned his forehead against hers, and she could sense rather than see his smile.

'Now I'm late,' he said, after what felt like an age but couldn't have been more than a second.

Eva bit her lip with a smile, unwilling to let the moment go just yet. 'Told you so,' she said, stifling a laugh.

Joss sneaked one last peck onto her cheek before he strolled out of the office with an irritating degree of calm and confidence.

When the door shut behind him Eva knew she couldn't avoid looking around her any longer. She glanced over the partition of her cubicle and saw that— as she might have guessed—all eyes had been on her and Joss. She waited for the inevitable jokey comments, but instead the women—and half the men—were looking at her wide-eyed.

Eventually her assistant blew out a slow breath in awe, and muttered something that sounded incredibly like, 'Lucky woman.'

If only she knew.

On the dot of six o'clock, Joss closed his laptop and reached for the jacket he'd chucked over the back of his chair. He'd promised Eva that he'd be done in good time for them to leave for his father's country house for the weekend, and he had no intention of breaking that promise. Especially after what had happened earlier.

What *had* happened?

He wasn't sure what had come over him. But as soon as he had walked into the office and seen her it had been as if something that had been missing for three days was suddenly back and in overload. As if he hadn't even known he needed something, and then was drunk on it.

It had been meant as a polite, friendly hello. The sort of public kiss that anyone would offer their fiancée when they'd been away for a few days. To do anything else would have looked suspicious. But as soon as their eyes had locked it had been so much more.

That night in Milan had come flooding back—everywhere that kiss might have led if they had decided to let it. And then it had been too late to back out, and he'd had no choice but to give in to what his body had been begging him to do. Let his fingers trace the soft skin on her jaw, let his lips brush against hers, setting off a chain reaction that was going to lead them somewhere dangerous.

Thank goodness they were in the office, with an in-built safety net of public scrutiny and didn't have to rely on their self-control. Or *his* self-control at least. Who knew? Perhaps hers was still rock-solid, and she'd only returned his kiss for show.

No, he knew her better than that, he realised. He had felt the passion in her, and the iron self-control that was holding her just as fast as it was him. She wanted him, but she wasn't going to let it get the better of her.

And now they were going to be spending a whole weekend together, holed up in an isolated country house. Most people would consider having their dying father there as having something of a chaperone effect—but, as he'd once said to her, they weren't 'most people'.

He had to stop overthinking this. It would only make them awkward. The only thing to do this weekend—if they wanted to keep the lie alive and his father happy— was to jump right in. Forget it was a lie. Live as if they were really an engaged couple, head over heels in love. And lust.

But where could that lead when sustained over a weekend? In Italy it had led to an aborted kiss, when they had both still had just enough self-awareness to keep it from going further. And—importantly—they'd had separate bedrooms to retreat to. When they found themselves alone behind a closed door with a four-poster in the corner how were they going to resist?

Well, they'd just have to find a way. Because the alternative was giving in to this attraction. Getting involved in something real. And he knew that if he let that happen Eva would get hurt—and he wasn't having that.

He opened the door to see that she was still sitting at her desk, concentrating on the screen of her computer, the pen in her hand tapping absent-mindedly at her lip. He couldn't look away, reminded of the feel of those lips less than a couple of hours ago. But she was obviously more aware of him than he realised, because she held up the pen in the universal sign for, *Give me a minute*.

She tapped a few more keys, and then looked up with

a beaming smile. 'Sorry—just had to get that done. Are we ready?'

He nodded, temporarily lost for words. He didn't know how she had that effect on him. But then, why would he? For years he'd been avoiding this. Avoiding finding out the effect that she might have on him. Well, there was going to be no getting away from it this weekend.

He wondered if she was as nervous as he was about them being in such close proximity. His father's house was far bigger than her flat, but there were fewer places to hide. Not when they couldn't drop their act as soon as they were inside the front door and start treating each other like indifferent colleagues again.

Eva wrapped a long scarf around her neck as she stood up, half an eye still on her computer before she finally shrugged her shoulders and shut it down.

'Problems?' Joss asked.

'No…nothing. I'd just hoped to be able to sort something out before we left. It's not a big deal.'

He held out her coat and she slipped her arms in while he resisted the urge to run his hands instead of the sleeves up her arms. To let them rest on her shoulders before brushing her hair aside and pressing a kiss at the nape of her neck.

Eva turned on the spot and was suddenly far, far closer than was comfortable. She barely had to look up to meet his gaze, and he resisted the sensible part of his brain that was urging him to take a step backwards.

'Ready, then?' she asked, glancing past him towards the door.

'As I'll ever be.'

Thankfully the drive out to the house was short and familiar—because, Joss thought, he really couldn't attest to his competency on the road with a car so filled with atmosphere.

His father had seemed chipper when they had picked him up, as Edward had slung his small bag into the boot of the car, but he had been asleep on the backseat within minutes.

'Everything okay?' Eva asked, after they had been driving in silence for another ten.

'Yeah, fine.'

He knew that he was killing any chance of conversation dead with his monosyllables, but for the moment he didn't care. The confined space of his car, with two people keeping secrets from each other, was more pressure than he could take.

It wasn't until he drew on to the driveway of his father's country house, between the old stone gateposts, that he finally felt himself start to relax. It wasn't so much that the pressure of having a fake fiancée was lessened. But out of the city, with space around them, it felt easier to breathe.

He parked close to the front door, and was relieved to see it open before they had stepped out of the car, and Thomas, their groundskeeper, pushing a wheelchair through.

Joss stepped out of the car and stared at the chair for a moment. He hadn't even realised that his father *owned* a wheelchair, never mind needed one. But Edward had slept the whole way here from London, and Joss suspected that he hadn't been entirely honest about how well he was feeling.

He waved at Thomas as he walked up to the steps at the front of the house. 'Thanks for this,' Joss said, gesturing at the chair. 'But he fell asleep while we were driving. We should probably just leave him a few minutes.'

'Probably for the best,' Thomas agreed with a nod. 'And this must be Eva.'

Joss looked behind him to see Eva stepping from the car, glancing briefly through the back window to check on his father. He felt a tug of tenderness at this obvious display of affection for the old man. He had no idea what the next few months had in store for them. How dark things were going to get while his father's body fought and then succumbed to this disease. But, however complicated things might be, he was glad that Eva was going to be by his side.

It was selfish, he knew, to look for her support. Especially when he knew that he wouldn't be able to return it. He was going to need all his strength to look after his father, to look after himself. And that was why he couldn't let this thing with Eva become real. Because she would get hurt.

He had to keep reminding himself of that. It didn't matter how good she looked, how incredible she smelled, how natural it felt to have her skin against his, her hand in his. Her life meshing with his. It didn't matter that it felt right, because it wasn't.

Except... That was not what Eva had said when he'd explained things to her. It wasn't what she believed. He had told her, plainly, the reasons he shouldn't be in a relationship, but they hadn't seemed to be good enough for her. He supposed he was lucky that she had her own reasons for wanting to stay single. Because she hadn't recoiled when he had told her of his depression. Hadn't blamed him when he'd told her about how his last marriage had ended. She had simply told him what he knew intellectually to be true: that he had been ill, and that what had happened had been out of his control.

Well, that might have been true then. But it wasn't now. He wasn't going to let this relationship get out of control. Because when that happened innocent bystanders like Eva got caught in the crossfire.

Eva walked towards him and threw a questioning glance towards Thomas. He loved the way she didn't even break her stride as she held out her hand to shake his. There was something in her posture, her confidence, her self-awareness, in the straightness of her back and shoulders, that he found completely captivating.

'Eva, this is Thomas. He looks after the house and the grounds. And perhaps he looks after my father, too, recently?' Joss said, glancing again at the wheelchair. 'Does he use this a lot, Thomas?'

'Ah...only now and then,' Thomas replied. 'More the last time he was here. He hasn't told you?'

'My father's been keeping secrets.'

'Well, he's not the only one, is he? It's lovely to meet you, Eva,' Thomas said. 'I hear that there are wedding bells in the offing. Congratulations to both of you.'

'Thanks,' Joss said, with a quick side-glance at Eva.

She was still smiling at Thomas, not showing any sign of discomfort at their lie. Once again he was blown away by her self-possession.

The sound of the car door opening behind them caused him to turn sharply on the spot, to see his father stepping out of the car.

'Sorry about that, folks. You know what it's like in the back of a car. Like being rocked to sleep in a cradle.'

Joss took the wheelchair from Thomas's hands and pushed it over to the car, but his father waved it away. 'No need for that, son. But if you don't mind I think I'll go and finish this nap inside. You show Eva around. Enjoy the last of the sunshine—it's been a beautiful day.'

Well, his father was right about that. The sun was low in the sky, casting long shadows over the garden through the leaves, which were just starting to turn shades of red and gold.

'Don't worry about the bags,' Thomas said. 'I'll get those. Your father's right. Go for a walk down to the village. The path's beautiful this time of year, and there's just enough light left.'

Joss turned to Eva with a questioning look, and she smiled. 'Good job I threw some boots in my bag. Sounds like a lovely idea.'

She pulled on her boots as she perched on the bumper of his car, and Joss watched his father walk slowly up the steps to the front door. It had only been a couple of days since he had last seen him, but his father seemed years older. And more sick.

When he reached Thomas he leaned on him for a few

moments before taking the last step up into the house. They would have to talk later. Have one of the difficult conversations they had all known must be coming about what his father wanted for the end of his life and how they could all keep him comfortable.

But for now the sun was just touching the tops of the trees, and he knew that the pub in the village would have good beer on tap. They could keep the real world at bay for an hour longer while his father rested.

He grabbed boots and a coat from the car and looked over at Eva, who was winding a scarf around her neck. Was she going to regret this in the weeks to come? Entangling herself with a man, a family, that was about to reach crisis point?

'Let's go,' he said, heading towards the path at the side of the house that would take them through the gardens and then down towards the village.

He walked quickly around the corner of the house, glancing up at the familiar red brick of the old building. This had never been his permanent home, but it had always been a happy place to escape at weekends and in school holidays. He knew every inch of the brickwork, every hollow and tree in the grounds. And soon it would be his, he realised. Along with the house in London and the dozens of Dawson's stores around the world. A whole portfolio of responsibilities was about to fall onto his shoulders.

'Is it far to the village?' Eva asked, catching up and walking alongside him.

'Not far—about fifteen minutes if we go down the

lane. If we want to stay for a pint we'd better walk the road way back. It'll be dark by then.'

'Sounds good to me,' Eva said, and they fell into silence as they walked.

Joss buried his hands deep into his pockets.

'Your father looked tired,' Eva said eventually. 'I'm glad he went for a lie-down. I was worried.'

Joss stopped for a second. 'Me too,' he said eventually. 'I should have expected it,' he added, walking on.

'Doesn't mean it wasn't a shock. Or that it won't be hard to watch.'

'I'm aware of that.'

As soon as the words were out of his mouth he regretted them. Or his tone, at least. He shouldn't be taking this out on Eva—it wasn't her fault. For a second he had a flashback to his marriage. Fights over nothing, and always with his dark mood at the start of them.

'I'm sorry, Eva. I didn't mean to snap.'

'It's okay. It's understandable,' she said, brushing a hand against his arm.

He shrugged it off. This was exactly what he was trying to avoid. Anyone being in the firing line if his depression came back. He was going to do everything in his power to stop that happening, but if he couldn't do that—if he couldn't beat it again—he was at least going to make sure that he wasn't taking anyone else down with him.

'It shouldn't be. You shouldn't let me get away with it.'

'You're under a lot of stress. I can't imagine—'

'Eva, don't make excuses for me. I don't need them. This shouldn't affect you.'

'If I didn't want it to affect me, Joss, I wouldn't have gone along with this whole charade in the first place.'

Joss turned to her, shaking his head and stopping his stride. 'That's different. Of course Dad being ill is going to affect you. But that doesn't mean that my moods should as well.'

Eva brushed her hand against his sleeve again, and this time he lost the battle to shrug it off.

'We're living together. I'm pretty sure that in a couple the other person's crappy moods are part of the deal. Trust me—give it a couple of weeks and I'll give you a run for your money.'

'We're not just talking about an occasional bad mood with me, though. This is something different.'

'Are you talking about your depression?' Eva asked. 'If you're telling me you think it's returning, Joss, then we can talk about that. We can think about getting you the help you need to get you through a bad patch. But snapping at people is something that we all do. It doesn't have to be a symptom of something bigger.'

'It's no excuse.'

'You're right.' She nodded. 'It's not. So apologise, think about what I've said, and we'll move on.'

'I'm sorry,' he said after a few long minutes of walking in silence. 'I don't want you to be brought down by this.'

'You know, maybe you could trust me to *tell* you when enough is enough. My happiness isn't your responsibility, Joss. I can look after myself. I always do.'

She was right—her happiness wasn't his responsibility. But he'd like it to be, he realised. He'd like his first task in the morning to be to put a smile on her face. He could think of a dozen ways right now that he'd like to try. And then he could spend his whole day keeping it there.

But another person's happiness was too big a responsibility on top of his own. Especially for someone like him, who had so spectacularly failed at the task in the past.

He also suspected there was more in what she said than first met the eye. She had always looked after her own happiness... Well, of course. Everyone had responsibility for their own happiness. But the way she'd said it—there was independence and then there was isolation. He suspected he knew which side of the coin she was on.

'So you always look after yourself?' Joss asked, brushing past some overgrown gorse, the thorns catching on his coat.

'No one else volunteered for the job,' Eva replied, with a flippant smile that didn't reach her eyes.

It was obvious that she didn't believe what she was saying. Which meant she was hiding something. After exposing so much of his own past, his own vulnerabilities, he suddenly realised how little he knew about her. And he hated how unequal that felt. Hated that she might be able to hold that over him. If he was exposed, then she should be too.

That was what was behind him needing to know more, he told himself. It wasn't that he had any other reason to want to know why she hadn't met someone and settled down already.

'Somehow I find that hard to believe,' he said. 'I have a suspicion that plenty of guys were interested and none quite measured up.'

'What makes you think that?'

'Oh, you know. You hear things.'

She gave him a sideways look that told him exactly how unbelievable she thought that was.

'Um… I think we've already established that you *don't* hear things. Try again.'

He shrugged. 'Fine—I'm guessing. Are you going to tell me I'm wrong?'

He watched her carefully, watched her eyes narrow and her forehead wrinkle as she thought hard. So he had hit on something, then.

'Why are you so keen to pair me off, Joss? You're not going to be one of those unbearable people who can't see a single woman in her thirties without assuming there's something wrong with her?'

He'd give her full points for deflection, but zero for accuracy. Well, if he'd hit a fault line it seemed to make sense to keep pushing.

'I don't know. *Is* there something wrong with you?'

Eva threw her hands up and picked up her pace, calling over her shoulder. 'So you *are* going to be one of those people? Great.'

He jogged a few paces to catch her up. 'I just wonder why you think you have to do everything by yourself.'

She slowed down again. 'I never said that I did,' she replied.

'No, but I've watched you. In the office. With me. You like to be in control.'

'So? Who doesn't?'

He gave her a meaningful look. 'But a relationship doesn't work like that, does it? Sometimes you have to give the other person a chance.'

She shook off his comment with a carefully neutral expression. 'Good job we're not *in* a relationship then, isn't it? We're just pretending—which means I don't need to change anything about who I am for you.'

'Right, because *that's* a healthy way to approach things.'

'So now I'm unhealthy? Is that what's wrong with me, or is there something else?'

He tried to reach for her wrist, slow her down, but she dodged away from him.

'I'm starting to think you're impossible—does that count?' he asked.

'Oh, sure—why not add impossible to the list as well? At least you don't have to wonder why I'm single any more. It should be self-evident by now.'

Oh, it was becoming that way. The way she deflected his questions. The way her arms had folded over her body, putting physical as well as emotional barriers between them. The way she was making every effort to appear as unavailable and unattractive to him as possible…

She wanted to be single—fair enough. Relationships weren't for everyone. He knew that. But he recognised something in the way she oh-so-casually brushed off the idea of being involved with someone. He recognised it because it was so familiar. It was the same brush-off he'd given his father for years when he asked if he'd considered dating again, giving married life a second chance. The same expression he'd doled out to concerned friends who asked if he wasn't lonely with his string of meaningless dates.

Something had happened to make Eva feel this way about relationships, and he wanted to know what it was.

'So have you always felt like this?' he asked, as the sun slipped behind the thick hedgerows, leaving them in a twilight that cast murky shadows across her face.

'Yeah, I suppose… Just never thought I'd be the settling-down type.'

'But you do date?' he clarified.

'Of course I date. I'm not a hermit.'

But why bother dating if you didn't want a relationship? He knew that one tended to lead to the other, which was why he had stayed clear of both.

'Why do you date?' he asked.

'I don't know—for fun? To meet new people? Do new stuff?'

'Why meet new people who you're not planning on seeing again?'

He could see from the tight expression on her face that he was annoying her. Well, good—if it meant that they got to the bottom of this issue and she stopped evading his probing.

'I see some of them again,' she said, a note of defiance—or was it simply irritation?—in her voice.

'What—two, three times, I'm guessing.'

'What is this, Joss? Are you stalking me now, or just planning to?' she asked as they reached the end of the lane.

He could see the lights from the pub across the road. They crossed to it in silence, and it wasn't until they were installed at the bar, each with a pint of real ale, that he picked up his line of questioning.

'I'm not stalking you,' he said, just in case she hadn't been kidding. 'I'm just guessing. But I'm pretty sure I'm right, or you wouldn't have reacted that way.'

She took a sip of her beer, and he could see the machinations behind her eyes as she tried to work out what his angle was. Why he was so interested.

'I just don't get why you want to know, Joss. Why it's any of your business, in fact.'

He managed a wry smile. 'You're right. It's not. I mean, if we were *friends* then it would be normal for us to talk about this sort of stuff—the guys you're dating, what you want for your future. But we're not friends.'

'We're not?'

'Of course we're not. How can we be when you're so intent on keeping me at arm's length?'

'Um… I thought we were keeping *each other* at arm's length? I thought we had decided that was the best thing to do? We both know that getting involved romantically is a complication this situation really doesn't need.'

'I'm not talking about romance, Eva. I'm talking about friendship. We've barely spoken since Milan. And I don't know about you but it feels weird to me. We're living together. We're working together. We're spending the bloody weekend together with my dad. If we can't even be friendly to each other it's going to be unbearable. And we don't know how long we're going to be keeping this up. Months in the same house but living as strangers—it just wouldn't feel right.'

'Now you're accusing me of not being friendly? You *do* remember we had this exact conversation the other day, except it wasn't me who was being standoffish.'

'You were talking about being friendly.' He laid a hand over hers, where it was fidgeting with a beer mat. He wanted her to focus on their conversation. He needed her to open up to him, and he didn't want to think too hard about why. 'I'm talking about being friends, Eva. Do you even know that there's a difference?'

'I have friends.' She shrugged his hand away with an annoyed flick of her fingers.

'Do you? Really? People you tell your darkest secrets to? Who know you as well as you do yourself?'

She looked up from the beer mat and met his eye—there was fire in her expression now, and he knew he was close to cracking her. Close to the truth.

'That's a pretty narrow definition of friendship.'

'I don't know… I think most people agree it involves opening yourself up. Being vulnerable.'

'Oh, and you're the expert on that, I suppose? Because you're so open to letting new people into your life. That's why you had to convince your assistant to pretend to be your fiancée rather than find yourself a real one.'

He choked on his beer and then looked at her for a few seconds without speaking. She was right. They had a lot in common—which meant he could tell her the truths he was pretty sure she needed to hear. It wasn't as if *she* was holding back. And she wasn't going to get out of talking about herself by turning the conversation to him. They'd already talked about his vulnerabilities—at length. He had no desire to go over that again.

'That's different. Other people got hurt. I'm protecting them, not myself.'

'You're *so* noble. The fact that you don't have to take a risk on anyone else—that's just a side benefit, I suppose?'

He reached for her hand again, hoping that the contact would bring her closer. Let her see that he was on her side.

'Don't turn this around. We were talking about *you*.'

'We were talking about vulnerability…about letting people get close. I think turning this around is pretty valid.'

'Fine, and we can talk about me later, if that's what you want. But right now we're talking about you. Why is it you don't want to let me in?'

CHAPTER NINE

'THIS ISN'T ABOUT YOU, Joss. It never has been.'

Her hand flew to her mouth as she took in a deep suck of air. She hadn't meant to say that.

Ever since he'd started digging, digging, digging—trying to get her to talk about why she didn't want to get involved—she'd told herself she shouldn't let him in. Letting people in never led anywhere good, and with Joss Dawson it would be downright dangerous.

It had been easier to dodge and deflect his questions when they'd been walking, with shadows to hide her face and the ability to walk off when he hit too close to the bone. But here in the cosy, intimate atmosphere of the pub, with the fire roaring behind them and Joss perching so close to her on a bar stool that she could see the golden flicker reflected in his eyes, she knew there was nowhere to escape.

The only way to shut this conversation down was to give him what he wanted—show him that a relationship wasn't an option for her, the same way it wasn't for him. Perhaps then he'd let the topic lie.

'Look, I know what it's like to have someone you

love leave you and hurt you, okay?' she said after a long pause. 'Is that what you want to hear? Because it's pretty much a description of my entire childhood. Both my parents in the army, taking it in turns to ship out while the other one was stuck at home with me. Me making friends and then being told we were leaving again. Until one day my mother didn't come home from her tour, and my dad—rather than be stuck with a grieving teenager—packed me off to boarding school so he could lose himself in his work. So for the love of God, Joss, don't talk to me about opening up. Some of us have perfectly good reasons for being happily closed books, thanks.'

She watched him as she waited for a response. Fine lines appeared at the corners of his eyes and a muscle in his jaw flickered. He was waiting, weighing, judging. Was he going to push further, or had she revealed just enough to make him back off?

'I'm sorry,' he said. 'I didn't know.'

Bingo. Well, her plan had worked, at least. But with the new information in the air between them, and old wounds exposed for the first time in years, she felt uncharacteristically vulnerable. Small and unprotected.

'It's fine. I just want to drop it now. We should change the subject.'

'Right.'

They sat in silence for a few minutes, while she tried to think of somewhere safe to take the conversation. Work? They had enough of that at…well, at work. His dad? That wasn't exactly going to lighten the mood. And there was no point waiting for Joss to pick up a small-talk baton. They'd already established he was all but incapable of that.

She glanced around them for inspiration and her eyes fell on a framed picture of the manor house, where they had left his father resting. Until she saw the picture, faded behind the bar, she hadn't really thought about the house as being part of the village, of Joss belonging to a community.

'So, has your family always owned the house?' she asked.

Joss's face relaxed immediately with relief at her opening small-talk gambit. Much as he had been pushing, it seemed he was as happy to see the personal topics dropped as she was. Perhaps because it meant that she wasn't turning the conversation back onto him, as she'd threatened.

'No, Dad bought it when I was small,' he said. 'After he and Mum divorced. He wanted somewhere in the country to bring us—get us out of the London fumes occasionally.'

Eva nodded slowly, raising her eyebrows. 'Well, when he wants to escape, he does it in style. How old were you when your parents split up?'

'Young enough not to remember it. It was all amicable. They're still good friends. No deep scars to probe there.'

'I'm glad to hear it.' She smiled, relieved the atmosphere really was lightening between them. 'So you used to come here at weekends?'

'And school holidays. You should see it in the summer—it's beautiful.'

'You're lucky.'

'I am.'

She could tell from the way he said it that he knew how incredibly privileged his life had been. But there was a tinge of sadness there, too. Because next time the house saw summer perhaps it would belong to Joss. And that could only mean one thing. She wondered whether Joss was making that same connection.

She finished her beer and glanced at her watch. 'Do you think your dad will have woken up?'

'Probably. We should head back anyway. I'm not sure whether Dad has asked Maria, Thomas's wife, to arrange dinner. But if he has you won't want to miss it.'

'Another woman who likes to cook for you—should I be jealous?'

Eva could feel a blush rise on her cheeks and turned her face to the fire so she could at least blame her colour on the heat from the flames. Thankfully Joss didn't capitalise on the potential of that sentence to get her confessing more secrets she didn't want to share.

'I'll drink up and you can find out for yourself.'

As they crunched up the gravel driveway towards the front door of the house Eva realised that there was one factor of spending the weekend with Edward they hadn't talked about yet—sleeping arrangements. Thomas had told them not to worry about their bags, which presumably meant that by the time they reached the house they would have been delivered to one of the dozens of bedrooms a house like this must contain—and, despite the copious number, they would have been delivered to the same one.

She could only hope that it contained an enormous bed, large enough for them to share without meeting in the middle at some point in the night. Or that there'd be an elegant chaise longue in the corner of the room that Joss could retire to in a show of gentlemanly manners.

If all else failed there were the flannel pyjamas— long legs and sleeves of course—that she'd packed just in case she found herself needing to protect her modesty.

They walked up the front steps and were met by Thomas at the door.

'How's my father?' Joss asked as soon as the door opened, and Eva couldn't help a small smile at his devotion to his father even in the sad circumstances.

'Still resting,' Thomas answered, with a concerned look. 'I've put you and Eva in your usual room, Joss, and Maria says dinner will be ready at eight. If you look in on your father, could you ask him if he'd like a tray instead and let me know? I think the journey must have taken it out of him.'

'Of course,' Joss said, his voice heavy with worry, and he gestured for Eva to go ahead of him up the stairs.

'Do you think he's okay?' Eva dropped her voice as they climbed, fearful of disturbing Edward, though with the treads carpeted in a lush, thick velvet, she supposed their voices wouldn't carry far.

'I'm shocked,' Joss replied. 'I didn't think that just driving to the country would tire him out so much. Either things are moving quicker than he expected, or he's not been telling the truth about what's going on.'

Eva had suspected as much herself. 'Are you going to ask him?'

'I already have. And I've offered to go to the hospital with him. He brushed me off with barely a word. He said he didn't want me dragged down by it.'

'Sounds like he wants to protect you.'

'Parents, huh?' A grimace crossed his face. 'Sorry, I didn't mean…'

'It's fine. You don't have to apologise for having a great dad. I just feel lucky that I got to know him too. You know, he's something of a father figure to me.'

'It will make him happy to know you think that.'

She shrugged, a little embarrassed. 'Well, let's not go telling him. We wouldn't want him to think we're getting all mushy.'

They reached the top of the staircase and Joss gestured her down the corridor in front of him. His steps slowed as they passed door after door, and eventually Eva had to laugh.

'My goodness—how many rooms *are* there in this house?'

'Last count? Fourteen bedrooms. And half as many bathrooms. Not sure about downstairs. I've never counted…'

'So, fourteen bedrooms and we end up—'

'Here,' Joss said, as they finally stopped and he opened the door.

Well, she'd been right about the chaise longue, at least. It was positioned under the elaborately draped Georgian paned windows, upholstered in a deep navy, with a pattern that caught the light from the chandelier overhead. A fire was set in the grate opposite the bed—a four-poster, naturally. It had a canopy up by the ceiling, and heavy curtains tied back in each corner. Crisp white pillows were piled up at the head of the bed, and instead of the sheets, blankets and eiderdown she'd been expecting there was a fluffy duvet, also covered in simple white cotton.

She turned to Joss and had to suppress a giggle.

'I know. It's a lot. But imagine a normal-sized bed in a room like this. You'd never find it.'

'No,' she said, shaking her head, her eyes wide. 'It's perfect. It's just…'

'Ridiculous? At least I drew the line at frilly sheets.'

'Yeah.' She let out a laugh. 'Yeah, a bit ridiculous.'

She crossed to the bed and had to do a little hop in order to hitch herself up onto the mattress. Joss came and sat beside her as she kicked her heels against the frame, and she turned to look at him, smiling.

'Here I was thinking it was going to be awkward, us sharing a bedroom, and I'm bursting out laughing as soon as we get in here.'

'Not what I'm usually aiming for when I show a woman to my bedroom,' Joss said. 'But I'll take it under the circumstances. You thought it would be awkward?'

'Well, of course. You didn't?'

'I hadn't really thought about it.'

'You're lucky to have me, d'you know that? To do your thinking for you. You really do need someone who knows how to do your job.'

'I never said I wasn't lucky.'

'Good. Let's keep it that way.'

She glanced around the room. Her comments on the decor and the house and the furniture had broken the ice when they'd entered the room but now, as they sat on the bed together she could feel tension mounting between them as they both looked around.

She presumed he was thinking the same thing she was—where were they going to sleep?

'I'll take the chaise longue,' Joss said eventually. 'I'll sneak some stuff from the linen closet.'

'And risk Thomas and Maria finding out that we're not what we say we are?'

'I'll blame it on you. Tell them you feel the cold,' he said, with a laugh that eased the tension again.

Eva pushed him gently on the arm. 'Throw me under a bus, why don't you? You know, the bed's the size of a continent,' she said. 'I trust you not to try anything if you want to share.'

'Wow. You have such a high opinion of me you feel you have to spell that out?'

'It was a generous offer and it comes with an expiry date. Just a warning.'

'Fine. Well I accept your offer.'

'Good.'

'Good.'

And all of a sudden awkwardness was back with a vengeance. She glanced across at Joss, then looked away as soon as she realised he had done the same. Being around this man was worse than being a teenager. At least then you could be pretty sure your crush was as messed up and confused as you were. But neither she nor Joss were hormonal kids. The decisions they made now would have real consequences over the coming days, weeks and months. There was no kissing now and then pretending it had never happened.

Except it was too late for that, Eva realised. Kissing without consequences was what they had tried in Milan, and if the tension between them right now was anything to go by there was no doubt that pretending it had never happened wasn't an option.

'I should check on my father,' Joss said at last, breaking the atmosphere between them.

It was a temporary reprieve; she knew that tension would be waiting for them when they climbed the stairs at the end of the night and found themselves locked in here until morning.

Joss disappeared for a few minutes, and then stuck his head round the door. 'Dad's going to join us downstairs, but I'm going to give him a hand getting ready. Do you need anything?'

She shrugged, and glanced pointedly around the room. 'Well, I didn't pack my tiara. Will I be needing one of those?'

'Oh, don't worry about it. Chuck on any old jewels. Kidding!' he added, when her expression must have shown her surprise. 'I'll see you downstairs.'

Eva descended the stairs, wondering how on earth she was meant to find the dining room without a map or a compass. When Joss had been trying to find her mews house he'd had the benefit of satellites and technology, but she suspected there wasn't an app for navigating your fake fiancé's country home.

She stuck her head around a couple of doors, revealing grand reception rooms with clusters of uncomfort-able-looking furniture. In the end she followed her nose down grand corridors to the back of the house, until the sound of Radio 4 came into hearing and the smell of roasting chicken grew stronger.

She checked another couple of doors until eventually she stumbled into a room with an enormous range cooker and an elegant woman—seemingly in her fif-ties, and certainly in charge—stirring something de-licious-smelling.

The door hinges squeaked and the woman turned around, her face lighting up with a smile. 'You must be Eva,' she said. 'I'm Maria. I try and keep this house in order and keep those men fed.'

Eva returned her smile, feeling instantly welcome. 'And you do a beautiful job of both, by the looks of things. Roast chicken?' she asked, knowing that food was always a safe conversation-starter.

'With lemon and garlic sauce,' Maria replied. 'Now, don't tell me that the three of them have abandoned you to find your own way here?' she said with a tut.

'Oh, Joss is—'

'Never mind what they think is more important. You're our guest. If I'd known they'd left you to wan-der the halls I'd have come and looked after you myself. Now, take a seat and tell me what you'd like to drink. Tea? Or something more appropriate to the hour? A little aperitif?'

'Well, I suppose a gin and tonic would go down well,' Eva said, after thinking about it for barely half a second. 'But only if you join me. The dangers of drinking alone and all that.'

'Oh, well, I think I probably should—seeing as I appear to be in charge of you. Right, then, let me find us a lime. I know there were some in the delivery yesterday.'

Maria disappeared for a couple of minutes and returned with two glasses filled almost to the brim with ice, lime and clear sparkling liquid.

'I'm sorry—I should have asked if you want this in the drawing room,' Maria said, her brow suddenly creasing. 'Edward asked me to set the table in the dining room for dinner, but he normally has a drink in here with us first. You can go through, though, if you prefer.'

'No, not at all,' Eva said, raising her glass in a salute to Maria and taking a long sip. 'A drink in here sounds perfect to me. It's ridiculously warm, for one thing.'

'Decision made, then,' Maria said, opening the door of the Aga and peering inside. She pulled out a perfectly golden chicken and placed it on the warming plate on top of the range before sliding a meat thermometer into the flesh.

'Can't be too careful,' she said, glancing over at Eva. 'With Edward's health being what it is. I've tried to get the rest of the house warm for him, but a heater in his bedroom and the Aga in here seem to be the only things that work.'

Eva didn't have a chance to reply before the door of the kitchen opened and Joss, Edward and Thomas all appeared.

'Ah, about time. You gentlemen abandoned poor Eva,' Maria scolded them. 'We both had to take some medicinal gin for the shock,' she added, with a wink to Eva.

'Excellent idea,' Edward said. 'Think I'll have one of those myself. Anyone else?'

He made to walk away from where he was leaning on Joss's arm, but stumbled with his first step. Joss helped him over to a chair instead.

'You sit down, Dad,' Joss said, sharing a concerned glance with Eva over the top of Edward's head. 'I'll get the drinks.'

By the time they were all seated formally in the dining room Edward was looking tired again, ready for another lie-down. Eva and Joss shared another concerned glance, but this time Edward caught the look between them.

'Enough, you two. If you've got something to say, then just say it. I'm having a tiring day. Not sure why, but I suppose it's to be expected under the circumstances.'

'We're just worried, Dad. You seem more tired than you were last week.'

'I *am* more tired,' Edward said. 'But my doctor's not worried. I called him, you know. I'm not just pretending this isn't happening. He said it's completely normal. I just need to rest more. Which means we should get this conversation done with so we can all eat and get to bed.'

'What conversation?' Joss asked.

Eva felt a shiver of foreboding. She could guess what conversation.

Edward reached for a folder of papers that Eva realised he must have stashed on a chair earlier.

'We need to talk about my will,' he said.

'Dad—' Joss tried to interrupt.

But Edward wasn't having any of it.

'No, son. We need to have this conversation at some point and I'd like to do it now, while I'm still well and no one can accuse me of having gone doolally or anything like that. Not that it matters much *what* you say, actually, because it's all finished already. I just thought you might like to know what's in there.'

Joss pushed his chair away from the table and Eva could see him glancing at the door, wondering if he could bail out on this conversation. He'd better not dare leave it to her—she'd make him pay if he did.

'Dad, it doesn't matter to me what's in there.'

'Well, it matters to me. So you can sit there and listen, if you're quite finished talking.'

Eva shifted uncomfortably in her chair. It was hard enough being caught in a family argument. When it was about a will, and it wasn't even your family, she was all for bolting for the door herself.

'Maybe I should leave you two…?'

'Not at all, dear,' Edward said when Eva tried to excuse herself. 'You're part of this family now, and I'd like you to stay. I know Joss will tell you everything anyway, so this way we save him the trouble. Right, I'm not going to go over every detail, because you know all the business stuff already. But the personal stuff we've not talked about before. It's not complicated, though. I'm leaving your mother a large amount of cash, so neither of us have to worry about her being comfortable for the rest of her life. But most of the rest of it goes to you, of course, Joss. Including the London house and this draughty old place. But the mews house is yours, Eva. It's been your home for many years, and I would hate to think of you having to leave it. I hope that you'll accept?'

'Edward,' Eva protested straight away. It was too much. Too generous. 'I couldn't possibly—'

But Edward shook his head defiantly. 'I don't want to hear anything like that. A simple thank-you would be fine.'

She couldn't accept. Of course she couldn't under these circumstances.

If Edward knew the truth about their fake relationship he wouldn't be doing this. It wasn't fair to let him make decisions like this based on a lie.

'Edward, you don't understand. About me and Joss—'

'No, no.' Edward said decisively. 'I'm quite sure that your relationship is none of my business. Really, Eva dear. This is a gift for you. Quite apart from what you and Joss mean to one another.'

She shared a long look with Joss, and tried to communicate what she was thinking without speaking.

Was he angry with her? She would tell Edward the whole ugly truth if she had to. This had gone too far. It wasn't fair on the sick old man. She'd gone along with his misunderstanding when he'd assumed that she and Joss were a couple because it had seemed a small thing to do to make him so happy. But this—this was different. This was legal—a binding contract and the transfer of property—making their little white lie suddenly seem a whole lot more serious.

'The mews house *should* be yours,' Joss said at last.

She wanted to kick him under the table for continuing to lie to his father. They should just tell him the truth. Come clean. She turned and glared at him.

'I mean it,' he carried on. 'I'd give it to you anyway, if it came to me. I'm serious,' he continued, when she widened her eyes at him, trying to get him to stop talking. 'Don't fight this, Eva.'

His voice was softer now, gentler, and she found she couldn't argue with him when he was being reasonable.

And when she thought of her mews house as being really her own... It meant that she would have a little piece of the city that was always there—a safety net whenever she needed it. She fought back tears as she rose from her chair.

'Thank you, Edward,' she said, walking around the table to give him a kiss on the cheek. 'It means the world to me. It really does.'

'Well, let's hear no more about it,' Edward said, his cheeks flushed a little pink.

Maria appeared at the door with such promptness it seemed inevitable that she had been waiting outside, listening for an appropriate break in the conversation.

'This looks delicious, Maria. Thank you,' Eva said as the platters of food were set down in the centre of the table.

With the difficult topic of the will set aside, they all relaxed into friendly conversation, though she could see that Edward's eyes were fighting to stay open halfway through their main course. She glanced at Joss, and saw that he had noticed it too. As their eyes met she felt a flash of connection between them, and knew that in that moment she could read him completely. She wondered if she was as open to him as he was to her. What he could see if she was.

A warmth started in her chest and sank to her belly as she realised how close they had grown over the past week. How she had really started to know him, with their communication becoming subtler, more personal, more intuitive.

She didn't want to think too much about what that meant. About the risk that she was taking in letting him in. Because that *was* what she was doing. Whether she had intended him to or not, he was getting under her skin, into her thoughts, into her life. And now, when she looked at him, she saw something familiar—something that had been part of her life for so long she would recognise it anywhere. She saw the void that he would leave when he left. She saw her life without him. The spaces she would have to try to fill when he wasn't part of her world any more. The voids that would haunt her at night and occupy her thoughts during the day.

She'd seen those voids around both her parents when she was growing up, and had wondered how her life would look if they were gone—really gone—and she was left behind. And then her mother had been killed on duty and she'd found out. She'd lived longer with the space that her mother had left behind than she had with her mother there. It was like a shadow in the corner of the room, reminding her of what she'd lost. What she'd never had much of a claim on in the first place.

And she could see that void around Joss now. See the hole that would be left in her life when this was over.

She'd never meant to let it get this far. It was meant to be a lie. Their engagement *was* a lie. But these feelings that she was having for him—they were very, very real.

She didn't know what to do with them. Her instincts were telling her to run. To get away from him now, while she still had a chance of plugging that space, of rebuilding her life without him in it. But her heart wanted her to stay. She knew that from the way it ached when she thought about leaving. About what they were going to do when they had to get back to real life. When she thought about a life without him in it—or, worse, a life where they were polite to one another in the office and then tried to forget each other existed the moment they left.

Joss frowned slightly, and she realised she had shown too much in her expression. Even if he couldn't understand the minutiae of the struggle she was feeling at that moment, he knew something was wrong. And she had a suspicion that he was going to expect her to explain herself later.

A clatter disturbed her thoughts, finally forcing her gaze away from Joss's, and she realised that Edward had dropped his knife. He'd barely touched his meal, but now he lay down his fork too, and took a sip of wine.

'I think I'm going to retire and leave you young people to enjoy the rest of the meal,' Edward said. 'I'm sure that Maria will have a delicious dessert in store, so please don't let it go to waste.'

She called goodnight to Edward as Joss took his elbow and helped him out of the room and presumably up the stairs to bed. Left alone, Eva wondered whether she should make her escape. But what would Joss think if he came downstairs and found her not at the table? And even if she decided she wanted to, she had nowhere to go.

She could escape to the bedroom, but Joss would be there as well soon enough. She might remember how to get back to the pub in the village, but what would Edward, Thomas and Maria think of her taking off in the dark? They'd know that there was something wrong between her and Joss, and that was the last thing she wanted for Edward just now.

Joss appeared at the door a few minutes later, and made her glad that she had stayed. His eyes looked heavy, as if he was fighting off emotion, and she knew he needed company. That if he were alone his thoughts and fears would torture him.

'Is he okay?'

'Tired,' Joss replied. 'He says he's not in any pain, but I'm not sure I believe him. I'll check on him later, and if he's not sleeping soundly I'll call the doctor. I'm sorry, Eva. I should never have brought you here. You shouldn't have to go through this. It's not fair on you.'

'I'm glad I'm here,' she said automatically.

But as the words passed her lips she realised that she meant them. Even if it *did* mean facing the sadness of watching Edward fade by the day. Despite her earlier thoughts of escape, she knew that this was important. That if she left these men to fend for themselves at this crucial time she would be hurting both of them, and she didn't want that.

It was dawning on her just how far she had let both of them in already. She had told herself after her mother had died and her dad had sent her away that she wouldn't do that again. She would never let anyone leave a hole in her life that she didn't know how to fill. But somehow the two Dawson men had found a way in.

Her affection for Edward was nothing new, but since he had given her the news of his illness, since her closeness with Joss, it had changed. He was no longer the kindly old boss she'd always thought him. He'd become more than that. He'd become like family.

And Joss? She didn't know *what* to think about Joss and how she felt about him. She had never meant to feel *anything* about him. She'd had a crush, yes. But that was all it had been. An appreciation for a handsome face and an enigmatic attitude. So how, in a matter of a couple of weeks, had he come to be so much more than that to her? How was he suddenly so much a part of her life, a part of *her*, that all she could see was the dark outline of the shape he would leave in her life when he inevitably left her?

What she wanted to know was what she was meant to do about it. She knew it was too late to turn back without getting hurt. Hurting was inevitable now. But she needed a plan to get through it when the time came to end their engagement.

'How can you be glad?' Joss asked eventually, rubbing both his hands on his face and then reaching for his drink. 'I'd rather be anywhere than here.'

'I don't think that's true. I think you're glad to be spending time with your father. And I'm here for the same reason you are, I suppose. Because it's important to be with your dad right now. And because it's hard to do that alone.'

'You're right,' he said, looking up and meeting her eyes with a look that might burn her if she wasn't more careful. 'But it's not just that. It's not that I want *someone* here. I want *you* here.'

'Because your father thinks—'

'For reasons that have absolutely nothing to do with my father. Believe me, Eva. What I'm talking about has nothing to do with him.'

He wasn't kidding. She could read volumes in his expression, and filial duty was nowhere to be seen.

She dropped her eyes, breaking their connection. If she hadn't, there was only one place that the conversation would go, and she suspected neither of them was ready to go there. Yet. *Ever.*

The door opened and Maria appeared with a trolley to clear their plates. They sat in silence as she worked, only occasionally glancing across to one another. When they eventually had *tarte Tatin* and *crème anglaise* sitting in front of them, on elegant white and platinum plates, Eva let out a long breath, determined to start a conversation with something completely non-controversial.

But as she grappled around for a subject she found she was coming up with nothing. Everything felt so loaded with Joss. Their work, their home, their families… They all led to conversations more deep and meaningful than either of them wanted right now. And she hoped to goodness they were beyond the point where they would have to talk about the weather for lack of anything else to say to each other.

She pushed a piece of tart onto her spoon, and let out a sigh of anxious relief when Joss eventually spoke.

'I hear it's going to be a nice day tomorrow.'

So that was where they were. She didn't know whether that made her want to weep or laugh, but at least the ice was broken.

'We should take your dad out,' she said.

'He'd like that, I think. He's always liked to walk in the gardens.'

They fell into silence again, and Eva concentrated on finishing her dessert, counting down the pieces until this awkward dinner would be over. And then, with a mouthful left on her plate, she asked herself what on earth she was doing. The longer she could make this last, the better. At least with six feet of solid mahogany table between her and Joss she was safe from making any huge, irrevocable mistakes. Once dinner was over her safety net would be gone.

She lingered over the last mouthful, and responded enthusiastically and gratefully when Maria asked if they would like coffee. But as she drained the dregs of the drink she knew she couldn't delay any longer.

'Do you want to go straight up?' Joss asked.

And, although she had been expecting it Eva still felt wrong-footed. If she said yes, would that make it seem as if she was desperate to get to their room, into bed with him? If she said no, what would he read into that?

But she could feel her eyelids growing heavy, despite the coffee. It had been an emotionally draining evening, and although it wasn't late she wanted a bed—whatever the dangers of sharing it.

'I think I will,' she replied, stifling a yawn that just thinking about sleep had produced.

'Can you find your own way up?' Joss said. 'I think I'll use Dad's study and just finish up a few things.'

Eva let out a breath, trying not to show how her body had instantly relaxed, relieved at his words.

'I'll be fine. I guess I'll see you in the morning, then,' she said, standing up from her chair.

They both stalled by the table for a moment, and for a second she was unsure what they were waiting for. A formally polite kiss on the cheek? A handshake?

In the end, she darted past Joss, the lure of an empty bed too much to resist.

CHAPTER TEN

JOSS LISTENED TO her climb the stairs, her footsteps elegantly measured despite the way she had darted past him out of the dining room.

He sighed at the thought of having to crack open his laptop and put in another couple of hours' work. Since this thing had started with Eva his schedule had been punishing, with him trying to keep himself busy and out of her way as much as possible. Keeping himself from temptation. And now, knowing he would be returning to a shared bed, not just a shared house, the temptation was stronger than ever.

He wondered whether she had felt it too. That connection when their eyes had met across the dinner table... He shook his head. Of course she had felt it. Something like that couldn't be one-sided. It was the very fact that they were both feeling the same way that gave the moment its energy. Its power. He had to be more careful.

He turned on the computer and pulled up the latest reports from his store managers, scrolling through them without really reading. Despite his earlier concerns over how he was going to shoulder his father's business with so little notice, he needn't have worried. The transition plans they had put in place had worked just as they were supposed to. And, although there was still some anxiety in parts of the business, mostly things were going well.

He forced himself back to the start of the reports and made himself read them properly this time.

When he was done, he glanced at the clock and saw that an hour and a half had passed. Eva had looked pretty tired when she had left the dining room, so surely it would be safe by now for him to go up to bed? Everything would be simpler if she was asleep, he told himself. He could just climb into bed and pretend he was alone. Goodness knew, the mattress was big enough for the both of them.

He climbed the stairs slowly, and remembered the sound of Eva's feet on the treads. Had she been feeling as uneasy as him? Wanting to put off the inevitable?

How on earth was he meant to get any sleep in the same bed with her? Maybe he should stick to his chivalrous guns and sleep on the chaise longue as he'd suggested. If anyone caught him, it could be easy enough to explain away. An argument. Snoring. A dispute over the duvet. A sudden conversion to a conservative religious order. Or just a reminder that their sleeping arrangements weren't anyone's business but their own.

Who was he kidding? Sleep was in short supply these days, and if it was going to be difficult in bed with a woman he was attracted to, it wasn't going to be any easier a few feet away, freezing cold, wishing he were closer to her.

He turned the handle of the door to his room slowly, trying to remember where the hinges squeaked and where the loose floorboards were. If he could get into bed without waking her, maybe he could do an okay job of pretending that she wasn't there at all.

Fat chance of that.

He crept through the door, opening it as little as possible, and saw that Eva had left a bedside lamp on for him. He smiled involuntarily at the small gesture of consideration; it was probably more than he deserved.

Her dark hair was spread on the pillow, shiny with just a hint of red, like a conker, in the warm light from the lampshade. He silently gave thanks that the duvet was plump enough to hide any suggestion of what her body might look like beneath the covering.

And then cursed when his brain reminded him that he'd already seen enough to give him plenty of sleepless nights. That day in his father's office. Pale skin and delicate lace. Pink silk just skimming over the curve of her back.

He shook his head and turned his back to her as he slid open a drawer, careful to ensure that the wood didn't stick and make any unnecessary noise. He pulled out a T-shirt and started unbuttoning his shirt, trying not to think about the fact that he was undressing with Eva barely a couple of metres away from him.

If she were to wake up, open her eyes, what would—?

No. He stopped himself. There was no way he could let himself finish that thought. It wasn't fair on Eva, who had offered to share the bed on the understanding that he would be a gentleman.

It wasn't fair on himself either. He needed sleep, and it would never come if he was thinking about Eva watching him undress…maybe moving to kneel at the edge of the mattress as she watched, and then reaching out to help…

He struck a hand against his forehead. He really had to get this under control, he thought, taking a couple of deep breaths. Usually control was not something he struggled with. Since his diagnosis with depression he had taken back control over his life, bringing order to all those areas he had let his illness take over. Structured goals and routine had woken him from the fog that had clouded him for too long. Focussing on achievable objectives, sticking to his plan—even when he didn't feel like it—that was what had got him better. It would be foolish to slip now, to give the power back to his untrustworthy emotions rather than the techniques that he knew worked for him.

He flicked the lamp off, gently pulled back the duvet and slipped between the sheets, gasping at their icy touch on his feet and legs. For a moment he was jealous of the thick cotton pyjamas he had helped his father into earlier, though he hadn't owned anything like that in his life. Even the T-shirt was an out-of-character nod to decency for Eva's sake.

He glanced at the fire in the grate; it was burning low and doing as little as the central heating was to warm the room.

He shifted on the mattress, stretching his legs and wondering how far he could spread out without disturbing Eva. He needed to know where she was so that he could be sure he wouldn't touch her by accident. He reached out a leg experimentally, and breathed a sigh of relief when it encountered only more shiveringly cold sheet.

He turned on to his side, stretching out his arm as he did so, and his hand encountered warm softness. He froze, but the sharp intake of breath from beside him told him all he needed to know. Well, he'd worked out how much space he had—not enough. Eva must have rolled over at the exact moment he had turned, and landed on his hand. The weight of her was soft and heavy, and as he gently flexed his fingers he had to stifle a laugh. Turned out she had better protection against the cold and their attraction than he did.

'Flannel pyjamas?' he whispered.

He felt a shudder of laughter against his hand in return.

'Are you kidding?' she muttered, her voice heavy and slow with sleep. 'Of *course*, flannel pyjamas. It's freezing in here.'

Her voice was not much more than a breath, and the intimacy of whispering in bed with her made him ache.

She shifted and he acted on instinct, wanting to keep her near. As she turned over to face him he drew her closer, so when she eventually looked up they were practically nose to nose. He ran his free hand down her arm, feeling the cotton soft and warm beneath his fingers. The sensation made him achingly hard.

Who knew? he thought. *Flannel.*

Eva sucked in a breath and he realised she was feeling exactly what he was. That she was as keyed up as him, and had the same reservations.

'Still cold?' he asked, testing the waters.

'I've got goosebumps.'

It didn't necessarily answer his question, but it made him throb with the need to pull her even closer. His hand was still trapped beneath the curve of her waist, and finally it was too much to bear. He slipped it under her, until his arm encased her completely and his fingers could brush against the indentation of her waist.

'Better?' he asked.

She took so long to reply he was scared she'd changed her mind. That he was losing her.

'Hot.'

When she eventually spoke he closed his eyes with a groan. She had to know what she was doing, saying that. It was an invitation—or an acceptance. He wasn't sure who was leading this little dance. And he didn't care, because now his other arm was curving around her waist, drawing her against him until she could be in no doubt about how hot *he* was feeling right this second.

He nudged his nose against hers, asking a question he was already pretty sure of the answer to.

He wasn't wrong. Her hand came up to cup his face and she pressed her lips softly to his. Barely a whisper of a kiss at first. He held still, his arms squeezing her to him. It killed him, but he waited. Waited to see if she'd change her mind, as she had in Milan. If she was still holding back. Doing the sensible thing.

But the noise that came from deep in her throat told

him this was nothing like Milan. Her lips found his again—harder this time, demanding a response.

So he responded the only way he could, by possessing her mouth with his, exploring the textures and contours of her lips. Brushing soft kisses, tasting, touching with his tongue.

His hands bunched the soft fabric of her pyjama top at the base of her spine, pulling it tight across her breasts and revealing a couple of inches of bare skin above her waistband. She gasped softly as he did so, and then louder when his hands slipped beneath the cotton, desperate to know the feel of her skin.

'Okay?' he asked breathlessly, drawing away from her for a moment. It felt like ripping away a part of his own body.

'Freezing!' she said, with a gasp and a laugh.

She reached behind her back for one of his hands and drew it between them, rubbing his fingers and his palm between her own, blowing hot breath onto cold skin. He shivered and it had nothing to do with the temperature of the room. She kissed his palm and her lips branded him.

He barely had time to recover himself before she slipped his hand beneath the covers, cupping it around her breast.

'Better?' he asked, barely controlling the shake in his voice.

'Warm,' she replied, pressing another kiss to his lips, snaking her arms around him. 'Good. *Really* good.'

And then her hands were on his back, exploring, pulling at his T-shirt, and he didn't care whether they were fire or ice—he just knew that he wanted them. Everywhere.

He sat up so he could pull his shirt over his head and Eva rolled beneath him. When he looked down he could just make out her features in the warm glow from the fire. Her eyes were closed, her face relaxed, her body open and languid beneath him. He pinned her with his elbows either side, dipping his head to tease at her neck and her collarbone with his mouth and tongue as he unbuttoned her pyjamas, one tiny awkward button at a time.

With each inch of skin that was revealed he dipped his head lower, determined to learn every inch of her. And as the last button came open he kissed her navel, revelling in her gasp of appreciation.

He hooked his fingers into the waistband of her pyjama trousers, barely able to let himself believe that this was really happening. But her fingers were in his hair, encouraging, demanding. And as he skimmed the fabric down her thighs he kissed her lips again, hard. Knowing that every second of this night would be burned into his memory for ever.

CHAPTER ELEVEN

EVA WOKE WITH a delicious fatigue in her muscles, her head so heavy she could barely lift it to turn her other cheek to the pillow. She fought against the fluffy cotton duvet, which had formed a cocoon around her face, and stretched out a toe. The sheets on the other side of the bed were cold.

'Joss?' she called into the still room, lifting her head and propping herself onto her elbows. She strained her ears, listening for water running in the bathroom or footsteps on the landing. Nothing.

She reached for her pyjamas, where they had fallen by the side of the bed, and shrugged her arms into the soft flannel, which had long since turned cold, abandoned on the floor. Pulling on socks, she crossed the enormous bedroom into the en suite bathroom, where there were signs of a hasty exit from Joss. His toothbrush had been flung on the side of the cabinet, his T-shirt was still in a heap on the floor.

But there was no note. No explanation of his absence. No apology.

Nothing to explain the huge empty hole he had left in their bedroom or the ache in her chest as reality sunk in.

He had left her, just as she had always feared he would.

What on earth had she been thinking, going to bed with him?

She hadn't been thinking at all. Or at least not with her head. She'd woken up to find Joss behind her in the bed and herself practically rolling into his arms. He'd laughed about her flannel pyjamas, and then she'd gasped and sighed as they'd had precisely the opposite effect to the one she had intended.

In Milan she had held back, certain that giving in to her lust for Joss would lead to disaster. But things had been different last night. She had already accepted that he had a place in her life. That, however he left it, he was going to leave a space behind that was going to be hard to fill. But the way he made her feel when they were together—it would be worth it. She had never thought she would find a man worth that risk.

And now he had walked away from her without even a word.

Had he at least regretted it when he'd shut the door with her sleeping soundly on the other side?

She felt tears prick at her eyes and turned away from the mirror, not wanting to see them fall. A thick dressing robe hung on the back of the door and she pulled it on, aware how even her heavy-duty pyjamas weren't managing to keep out the chill.

She left the bathroom and glanced at the fireplace. She had no idea how to get any heat back into those dying embers, so she pulled the fabric of the robe tighter around her, holding her breath to avoid Joss's lingering scent trapped in the collar. Dropping on to the chaise longue, she glanced out of the window.

No sign of Joss's car—just neat parallel lines in the gravel leading away from where he had parked it yesterday. A shadow. A reminder that he had been there.

Eva shook her head, trying to shake off the gloom that had settled over her since she had woken in an empty bed. Was she overreacting? She hadn't even checked her phone. Her thoughts had flown straight to her parents—the way they had left her, as they always had. Her fears that anyone else she loved would do the same. She was going to feel pretty bloody stupid if there were half a dozen messages from Joss, explaining what was going on.

She crossed to the bedside table and picked up her phone, checking the screen. Nothing.

Well, she had never sat around waiting for a guy to call before, and she didn't much fancy starting now. She dialled Joss's number and felt her heart-rate jump when it started ringing. Once, twice—and then the voice-mail kicked in.

She frowned. It hadn't rung long enough for it to have redirected automatically. But the fact it had rung at all meant it was turned on. Which meant that he had to have rejected her call. He had seen her name flash up on the screen, known that she had woken without him, and then rejected her call rather than explain himself.

Nausea rose in her belly as she realised that he had really meant to abandon her. To leave her with no explanation at all. She fought the sickness down, forcing herself up from the chaise longue and formulating a plan for what to do next. She found her suitcase in the bottom of the wardrobe and started throwing things into it. If Joss didn't want her here—and he couldn't have made that much clearer—then fine. She would go.

She had tried and tried with her parents, had carried on loving them when they'd left her time and time again. And she had ended up with her heart broken. She had learnt her lesson—there was no point sticking around to let Joss do it to her again. She would get away and make a head start on building those walls she would need in place next time she had to face him in the office.

Eva jerked upright at the sound of footsteps on the landing, but it took only a split second for her to realise they were too light to belong to Joss. The gentle knock at the door confirmed her suspicions.

'Come in,' she called out, and knew before the head poked around the door that it must be Maria on the other side.

'I thought you might like some coffee,' Maria said, shoving the door open with a tray and setting it down on the table beside the chaise longue. 'And Joss asked me to fill you in on what happened last night.'

Mortification spread through Eva's veins. What on earth had Joss said to her? Had he told her what had happened? That they had slept together for the first time?

Then the reality of her situation started to sink in. No, Maria wasn't here to talk about what had happened between them in bed; she was here to make Joss's excuses for him.

Eva had fallen asleep last night, satisfied and safe in his arms. And at some point, when she had been reliving their passion in her dreams, he had sneaked away and arranged for Maria to do his dirty work.

'He didn't want to wake you or worry you,' Maria said.

From the hesitation in her voice, Eva guessed she wasn't any happier about the position Joss had put her in than Eva was.

Maria didn't know the half of it, she thought. Leaving unannounced was ungentlemanly at the best of times. In the middle of the night, following the first time they'd made love, when Joss knew exactly how big a risk she was taking on him... She didn't want to say it was unforgivable, but that was certainly how it felt right now.

'Edward was taken ill,' Maria said. 'We called the out-of-hours doctor and he called an ambulance. He's going to be in hospital for a few days.'

Eva nodded slowly, taking this news in. Perhaps she should have guessed that something like this had happened. She tried to get her head around the news and work out where this left her and Joss. So he had had a good reason for leaving. But none, she could see, for doing it without saying goodbye. Without a quick kiss and an explanation.

Had it not occurred to him that she would want to support him? That she would want to be there for him and Edward—especially when things were tough?

And it didn't explain why he'd rejected her call. Why

he'd not found the time in the last however many hours to drop her a quick message, letting her know what had happened. It seemed he had found time to keep Maria informed, after all.

Her heart ached for Edward, and for Joss watching his father fade. But it ached for herself as well. For the trust she had finally managed to put in Joss, only to see it trampled. To find herself abandoned, with her worst fears coming true.

She went to the tray to pour some coffee, wanting something to focus on.

'I'll leave you to your breakfast,' Maria said, her voice kind, and Eva guessed she had picked up on her distress even if she didn't know the cause.

As Eva sat and drank her coffee she wondered whether she was overreacting. Joss was at the hospital. Perhaps it had just been an inconvenient moment for her to call.

She watched the screen of her phone, wondering if he would call back, and then remembered that she was far too old to be playing those sorts of games.

CHAPTER TWELVE

JOSS REACHED INTO his pocket for his phone, and guessed before he looked at the screen that it was Eva calling. He was tempted to fire it off to voicemail again, as he had the last time, but knew that there were only so many times he could do something so cowardly.

As he had sat by his father's bedside last night he had gone over and over his decision to leave without waking her. He had taken his phone out of his pocket and replaced it again, wondering what he could say that would lessen the blow of her waking up alone in the morning, knowing he had left without a word.

It couldn't be undone now. He could apologise, explain that it had been an emergency, he hadn't wanted to worry her.

But he didn't want to lie.

The truth was he hadn't been thinking at all. He had been acting completely on instinct—looking after his father, looking after himself. And that was what worried him the most. Because in a time of crisis his selfish instincts had led to Eva getting hurt.

He'd not taken the time last night to think about how

his actions might affect her. It was what he had been afraid of all along—his selfishness. His instinct to look after his own needs was evidently incompatible with a relationship. They had only tried it for one night, and already Eva was paying the price. He had to put a stop to this before he did any more damage.

'Eva?' he said, hitting the green button on the screen.

'Hey,' she said, her voice neutral, flat. 'How's your dad?'

'Better, thanks.'

So Maria must have let her know what had happened. At least she had opened with a topic that he knew how to talk about. He could give her the facts, repeat what the doctors had said.

'They've made his breathing more comfortable. He'll be discharged in a couple of days. Maybe even tomorrow.'

'That's good news.'

He waited as the silence between them grew awkward.

'Can I come by and visit?' she asked.

The question was inevitable, but his answer had to be more than that. It had to protect her, to show her that they had got too close last night and needed to find some safe space between them again.

'That's not a good idea,' Joss said. 'He's still very tired. He's been asleep most of the time.'

'Okay,' Eva said, and they fell into silence again.

He thought back to being in bed with her, how they had moved and sighed and breathed as one body, and wondered how it was that intimacy like that could be lost. Easily, he realised, when one of you had walked away with no care for the damage they were causing. This wasn't something that had happened *to* them. It was something *he* had done.

'I'm sorry I had to leave in a hurry.' There—the apology was out. 'If you want to go back to London...' Joss continued, not sure whether or not he wanted her to take the hint, to be gone when he was eventually able to leave the hospital.

'I'll book a taxi to the station,' Eva said, and this time she couldn't hide the slight shake in her voice, that little tell of emotion.

He was doing it again. Being responsible for another person's emotions was too much. The people he loved were always going to be disappointed. Always going to get hurt. Even when he was trying to protect Eva, everything he did just meant she got hurt. It was better to end it now, like this, he told himself. The sooner he did it the better. He'd proved last night—to himself as much as to her—that he wasn't relationship material. If he didn't do this now, he was only going to end up hurting her more in the long run.

On Monday morning Joss pulled his car up to the front of his father's London house and rested his elbows on the steering wheel. Was it two days ago that he had done the same journey in reverse with Eva, or three? With the bright fluorescent lights and the constant noise of a busy hospital, it was hard to tell how much time had passed. Perhaps it was only two nights that he had spent sleeping uncomfortably in a straight-backed chair, aching to be home, to be back with Eva.

Except he'd known she wouldn't be waiting for him at the country house—not when he had all but told her to leave. And he couldn't go back to the mews. It wouldn't be fair to pick up as normal when he knew that they both needed to back off—for Eva's sake.

He'd not called her again. It was spineless, he knew, avoiding her hurt and recriminations like this, but what more was there to say? He didn't need her to tell him how badly he had acted. But now his father had been discharged, and they were back in London, he knew he couldn't put it off for ever.

He would have to see her at work. Tell her that they had to stop this. See if he could persuade her to keep up the pretence to his father, but forget that incredible night had ever happened. He wasn't sure how she was meant to do that—not when his own efforts had been so dismal. But they had to try.

He settled his father in bed and headed down to the kitchen to make them both a drink. When he returned, he eased open the door to his father's bedroom slowly, not wanting to wake him if he'd fallen asleep. But Edward was sitting up in bed.

'I thought you were going straight to the office?' Edward said, his eyebrows high with surprise.

'There's no hurry. I want to make sure you have everything you need first.'

Nothing to do with wanting to delay the inevitable confrontation, he told himself.

'From the way you crept in here, you thought I was sleeping—not likely to need much, in that case.'

So his father could see through him. Could see he wasn't telling him everything even if he didn't know the details of the evasion.

'It doesn't matter,' Joss said, refusing to engage with his father's probing. 'The office can manage without me for one morning.'

'And what does Eva think about this?' Edward asked.

Joss tried not to let his emotions show on his face, tried to keep his voice light. His dad was like a dog with a bone when he got an idea in his head. He wasn't going to be able to shrug his way out of this, he suspected.

'She didn't drive back with us.' Edward continued his line of questioning. 'I take it she left while I was in hospital?'

'One of us needed to be in the office,' Joss said. 'But she sends her love. I'm sure she'll visit soon.'

'Of course.' Joss could tell from the tone of his father's voice that he knew he had hit a fruitful line of questioning. 'Everything okay there?' he asked with fatherly concern. 'With you and Eva, I mean.'

'Of course it is,' Joss said, not wanting to worry his dad with the problems in his fake relationship.

He wished he could sound more convincing, but the truth was that things between him and Eva had never been worse. And their lie was meant to be making their father happy, not making him worry about them.

'I know all this must be putting a strain on things,' Edward said, reaching across to the chair beside his bed and patting the seat.

Joss sat down stiffly, recognising an order when he saw one.

'It's bound to. It's normal to have problems. Do you want to talk about them?'

'We're not having problems, Dad.'

He felt a wrench in his gut at lying to his father. Except he didn't even know at the moment what was a lie and what was true. He and Eva had started as something pretend, but this pain he was feeling—this was real. More real than anything he had felt through his actual marriage.

'And if you were you wouldn't talk to your old man about them anyway, isn't that right? I've been here before, Joss. Watching you struggle, keeping things to yourself. I don't want to do that again. I wished there was more I could do to help last time. I don't want to die wishing the same thing all over again.'

Joss dropped his head into his hands. 'I never knew you felt that way. I know I let you down with the divorce...'

Edward reached out and took his hand. 'Whatever gave you that idea? It broke my heart to see you struggling and not be able to do anything to help. But you have *never* let me down, son. You recovered, and now you have the opportunity to be happy. Please don't waste it.'

He couldn't lie to his father any more—even for his own good. He couldn't go on letting him think he was something that he wasn't. There had been too much unsaid between them over the years. Too many truths hidden.

'This is different, Dad. I'm sorry. Me and Eva—'

'You haven't told me everything about your relationship. I know that. I'm not simple, Joss. I don't need the details, because it's clear that you two care about each other very much. I think that was clear to me before it was to you. You love her, don't you?'

Joss didn't know what to say. He had tried so hard to convince himself he didn't—that it would be better for Eva if he didn't. But he couldn't lie to his father—not after what he had just told him.

'Yes. I do.'

'Then I want you to go to her and tell her that. And no matter what is happening with me, or what is happening with the business, I want you to remember to tell her that often. Okay? Nothing is more important.'

Joss wished it were that simple. That loving her would be enough.

CHAPTER THIRTEEN

EVA'S BACK AND cheeks ached with keeping her spine constantly straight and her expression neutral as she ghost-walked her way through Monday morning in the office, determined not to let memories of Joss break her perfect composure.

She'd been there since before the sun was up, and the streets were still quiet. If anyone had asked she would have chalked her early start up to commitment and professionalism, rather than the fact that she'd woken at five and been unable to bear the silence of her empty house any longer.

It was just the change back from the big, staffed country house to her little mews that had her spooked, she told herself. Nothing to do with the fact that the house didn't feel quite so much like a home now without Joss in it. Without knowing whether he had any intention of coming back to it.

She was completely in limbo. She hadn't spoken to him for three days, but as far as their colleagues were concerned they were still engaged. *Were* they still engaged? Or as much as they had ever been, anyway? She just didn't know. And it wasn't as if she could ask.

Under normal circumstances she would have no problem asking the man in her life what he thought was going on between them, but these were about as far from 'normal circumstances' as you could get.

As the last person left the office for lunch she let out a long breath and pulled in a lungful of air. It felt like the first she had taken in days. Her shoulders dropped from where they had been up by her ears, and as she tapped away at her keyboard she felt the rest of her body follow their lead and start to relax.

Which was why she jumped when she heard the all too familiar tread of his footsteps behind her, spookily loud in the silent office. She froze where she sat, fingers still on the keyboard. Taking a deep breath, she sent it to her shoulders again, forcing them into a state of relaxation that she didn't genuinely feel but she hoped would look convincing.

She turned slowly in her chair, delaying the moment when she would have to face Joss, lift her gaze to meet his. When she eventually did, anger and sympathy warred within her.

He looked like hell.

It was clear from the black bags under his eyes and the deep lines on his forehead that he hadn't slept properly since she'd seen him last, but worse than that was the expression of pain so clear in his features.

He'd obviously been going through hell. And he'd chosen to go through it alone rather than let her into his life and trust her to support him. To be there for him.

'We need to talk,' he said, his voice cold.

Her blood ran colder as she thought he must have terrible news about Edward. But she followed him through to his office and closed the door behind them.

'How's your dad?' she asked, bracing herself for the worst.

'Better,' Joss said. 'Home now.'

The air left her in a rush of relief, and she collapsed back into one of the chairs by his desk. 'Oh, thank God for that. From your face, I thought you were coming to tell me that he'd…gone.'

Joss sat beside her his expression still grim. 'No, he's home now. That's not what I need to talk to you about. It's us.'

All of a sudden she felt that chill again. The hairs on the back of her neck prickled, and she had a sudden premonition of where this conversation was going. Or where Joss thought it was going, at least.

'What happened on Friday night—it was a mistake, Eva. I should never have let it go that far.'

'Let it?' she asked, not able to keep the note of derision out of her voice. 'I don't think you were *letting* anything happen, Joss. I think you were making it happen. We both were.'

He leaned back against his desk and looked straight at her. She felt a shiver go through her at the emptiness in his expression.

'Then that was the mistake. However it happened, Eva, it was wrong.'

Surely he couldn't feel as blank as he looked about that night. She hadn't imagined the intimacy they had shared, or the ecstasy they had found together. And she wasn't going to let him repaint it all as flat and empty just because he had got scared.

'It felt right to me,' she countered. She knew she hadn't been alone in thinking that. Not at the time at least. 'It felt pretty good for you too, if I remember. I know you, Joss. You can't fake that with me.'

'How it felt isn't the point,' Joss said, refusing to engage with her. No eye contact. No acknowledgement that what she was saying was spot on the truth, whether he wanted to admit to it or not.

Eva stood and took a step towards him, planted her hands on her hips and forced herself into his line of sight. No hiding.

'It felt right, Joss, because it *was* right. There's something between us, and I know that you know it. Whatever it was that spooked you, that has you scared and running from this connection, we can talk about that. But I will not stand here and listen to you talk about it like it meant nothing. Like I mean nothing to you.'

'I want it to be nothing, Eva. It shouldn't have happened. I wish it never had.'

The words were so unpolished, so simple, it was impossible to hide from their blow. Eva felt the blunt impact square in her chest, and had to fight not to look defeated.

'And that's why you left me—even though you knew how much that would hurt me? This is because of your divorce, isn't it?' she said, deciding that nothing short of tackling this head-on was going to get through to him. 'Your depression.'

'This is because of *you*. Because I don't want you to get hurt.'

Oh, so noble while he was breaking her heart.

'Then don't hurt me again.'

It was as simple as that. He could give up on them now, walk away as if this connection didn't mean anything to him. Or he could try again, face his past and his fears, and vow to make his future different. He could accept that this depression might return, but that if it did this time he'd find support in a relationship, rather than seeing it as a burden.

'I'm trying, here, Eva. I'm not standing here saying this because it feels good. Or because I've somehow forgotten everything that happened on Friday night. It's burnt into my memories and my retinas and my skin and I'll never be rid of it. I'm doing this for *you*. Because I want to protect you.'

'And I'm meant to stand here and take it? While you push me away when we both know that we can make each other happy? I'm sorry, Joss, but no deal. You're going to have to try harder than that.'

She didn't know where it was coming from, this fire inside her. When she had woken to that empty bed, that empty room, that empty heart, she had been sure that this was over. That nothing Joss could say to her would make up for what he had done.

But as the days had passed she'd realised she was angrier about what he was doing to their future than what he had actually done the other day. If she'd had another chance with her mother she knew she would have jumped at it. She wouldn't walk away just because she had been hurt once. She would keep trying, keep fighting to keep the ones she loved in her life.

'I didn't want to hurt my ex-wife, Eva, and look what happened,' Joss said. 'I don't want the same thing happening to you.'

'I *know* what happened.' She took a step away from him now, raising her voice and throwing her arms up— anything to try and get through to him. 'You got ill, and your behaviour while you were unwell was a symptom of the disease. When you recognised that you saw a doctor and you got better. It's sad—of course it is—that by the time you realised what was happening it was too late for your marriage. But last time I checked permanent celibacy wasn't prescribed for depression.'

'There isn't a cure.'

Joss's voice was still infuriatingly flat and she stilled for a moment, studying him, looking for any sign of the man she had spent that incredible night with.

'Perhaps not. But there's treatment. There's hard work. There's support, if you'll accept it. Most importantly, Joss, there are second chances, and they're generally not to be sniffed at. I want to be with you. I want to try loving you. Believe me, I'm going into this with my eyes wide open.'

Joss met those eyes now, staring her down. Maybe using the L word had finally got through to him.

'The last few days—'

'Have been pretty terrible. It's taken a while for me to feel ready to have this conversation. To forgive you. Believe me, if you'd asked these questions on Saturday you would have got a very different reaction.'

'The one I deserved?'

'Probably. But this is the one you're getting now. I'm not letting you off the hook, Joss. I'm not going to be complicit in you walking away. If you want to break this relationship you're going to have to try harder.'

'I'll end up hurting you again. You know it's true.'

'Would you stop talking in prophecies, Joss?'

Ugh! If she didn't feel so frustrated she'd be close to giving up on him and his fatalism right about now. There were only so many rejections her ego could take, and whatever that number was they were getting dangerously close to it. She was going to walk out of this office with dignity, whatever Joss decided. So this was it. All her cards on the table. Then Joss could take it or leave it.

'Yes, you might do things that hurt me,' she started. 'You'd be a saint if you got through any sort of relationship without occasionally doing that. I'm pretty sure I'll hurt you too. Soon, actually, if you don't start listening to me rather than talking at me. A relationship comes from moving past that. Recognising that you've done something wrong, apologising for it and trying harder next time. If you're willing to do that, Joss, then I'm still game. Because, quite frankly, I can't imagine how I could walk away from this—from you—now.'

She stood watching him as he remained leaning against his desk, still scowling, still silent. Then he looked up and met her gaze.

It was clear to see how conflicted he was. There was something about the expression around his eyes that reminded her of how passionate he'd been that night, when he'd had her beneath him in his arms, ready and wanting him. But there was a tension in his jaw that she knew meant he was still fighting it. That her words hadn't had the effect she'd wanted. He was still afraid—of himself, not of her.

'This is a lot to take in,' she said, her voice hard but not angry. 'I cleared your diary for the day. I didn't expect you to be in the office at all. Why don't you go back to the house? Rest. You look like you've not slept for days. We can talk again later.'

He ran a hand through his hair and glanced at his watch, as if it held magical answers. 'You're right. I need to sleep.'

He stood upright and took a couple of paces towards her. He was about to step past her when he stopped, laid a hand on her cheek, and she drew in a breath, wondering if everything had changed in that last fraction of a second. But when she looked up she saw from his expression that he was still holding back.

He stroked her cheek with his thumb, and Eva had to resist the urge to turn her face into the warmth of his hand. She had made her position perfectly clear; it was up to him to come closer if that was what he wanted.

'I'm sorry for hurting you,' he said.

His voice trailed off and she knew he wasn't ready yet. He didn't understand his own feelings enough to share them with her.

She pressed her lips gently to his, cutting him off before he could undo what he had just said.

'That's a start.'

CHAPTER FOURTEEN

JOSS WATCHED EVA leave his office with the touch of her lips still burning on his mouth.

She made it sound so simple. As if everything they had felt the night they'd slept together was enough to base a relationship on. As if that were enough to cancel out what he had done afterwards.

It wasn't just that he'd left. It was that he'd cut her out completely. He hadn't been able to bring himself to talk to her on the phone, knowing that just the sound of her voice would make his resolve crumble. He'd kept it up for three days, falling back into old habits and isolating himself.

When he'd walked into the office and seen her sitting there, clearly aware of his presence, his breath had frozen in his chest. Waiting for her to turn around and look at him, he had felt every emotion he had been trying to bury over the last few days flood back, hitting him with a tidal wave of longing.

And then she'd been so angry, so fierce, and so sure of what she had been saying it had been impossible to argue with her. He'd walked into the office convinced that the best thing he could do for her was get as far away as possible—emotionally, at least, even if they couldn't manage it physically. It had never occurred to him what *she* might want. That she might be prepared to give him another chance.

He thought back to the dark days of his marriage. All the times his wife had tried to offer support and he'd thrown it back at her. Retreated more and more into himself, telling himself it was for the best, that he was protecting her. And where had that led them? She'd been hurt, and he'd had to carry the guilt of that. Was he just repeating himself now?

He turned the corner to Eva's mews and looked up at the big picture window of her apartment. He'd been looking forward to getting back here, he realised. It wasn't his own home he had been wishing for when he'd been trying to sleep in that crippling hospital chair. It had been Eva's. And he wasn't so stupid to think it was the bricks and mortar he'd been missing.

Nor was it her delicious body in his bed, because a sturdy wall separated them in this house. No, it was just *her*. Being close to her. Sharing his life with her. That was what had made this feel like his home.

He traipsed up the stairs and into the bedroom, shedding his jacket and shirt as he went. By the time he reached his bed he was down to his underwear and he collapsed onto the duvet, letting his muscles relax, finally, into the bed.

As his eyes drifted closed moments from his conversation with Eva back at the office drifted through his mind until one caught at him—*I want to try loving you.*

Not the first time he'd heard that word today. He'd told his father that he loved her, but he hadn't told Eva.

And in the moment when she'd all but told him she loved him too, he'd been so intent on telling Eva what he thought she needed to know that he hadn't listened to her. Her words hadn't reached him somehow. But he was listening now. *Did* she love him? Was that what she had been trying to say?

He couldn't stop the broad smile that crossed his lips as that thought sank home. It should have been scary. It should have set off warning beacons and alarms and flashing lights. Instead it filled him with warmth, a feeling of fullness that he couldn't remember ever having before. It filled him with hope.

And as he drifted into sleep he suspected that his world had changed.

He awoke to the sun low in the window, and creases from the pillow on his face. He'd fallen quickly and easily into sleep—something that had been a trial ever since his father had given him the news of his illness. His body felt refreshed and his mind was energised, full of Eva—still going over everything she had said to him at the office. Every retort to his omens of doom. Every argument against his careful reasons why they shouldn't be together.

She actually wanted to do this. She knew the risks. She knew who he had been before. She knew that the situation with his father could only ever get worse. And she still wanted to try.

The smile that had formed on his face before he had fallen asleep was fixed in place now, because he knew what he needed to do. He couldn't let her go. Not when he felt like this. She had put everything on the line for him, told him exactly how she felt, and he owed her the same in return.

He pulled on some clothes and went through to the kitchen, pulling open the fridge and glancing in cupboards. He was certain Eva would be able to create something from what he could see, but it was definitely not his forte.

He pulled out his phone and placed a call to one of his favourite restaurants, and arranged for them to deliver something worthy of Eva's palate. With glasses and cutlery and a nice bottle of red in hand he went through to the other room and laid the table, and then dug around in drawers to find candles for every surface. If he was doing this, he was going to do it properly.

She deserved that.

She deserved everything from him.

She had shown faith in him when he had deserved it least. When he hadn't even had faith in himself. And for once he believed her more than he believed the voices of self-doubt in his head. The voices that told him he was better off alone. That no woman deserved to have to put up with him again.

He was curious too. She had seemed so strong when she was talking to him back in the office. But he knew she feared being abandoned. That it was something that had haunted her life. And then, when he had gone and done it—had left her as she had feared—she'd seemed to come out of it stronger, rather than more shaken.

A knock at the door told him the food had arrived,

and he jogged down the stairs, returning a few moments later laden with foil containers. He placed them in the oven, as instructed, and then glanced at the clock. Quarter to seven. She could be home any minute.

He had barely sat down when he heard her key in the door downstairs. He jumped up and glanced around the room to make sure he had got it right. Candles flickered, reflected and refracted in the glass of the windows. The music was low and atmospheric. And the smells coming from the kitchen rivalled anything that Maria or Eva had rustled up for him.

There was nothing more he could do to prepare. It was time for them to talk.

'Something smells good,' he heard Eva call as she reached the top of the stairs and her footsteps turned towards the kitchen. She appeared in the doorway, and he stood completely still as her eyes widened when she took in the table and the candles.

'You've been busy,' she said, and he could tell from the careful modulation of her voice that she was taking care to keep her tone even. She wasn't going to give anything away, then. Wasn't going to make this easy for him.

'I might not cook, but I can order as well as anyone,' he said, trying out a smile, wanting to break the tension between them.

This afternoon he had been so sure this was right that he had forgotten how the tension in the atmosphere ratcheted up when he and Eva were in a room together. It was never going to be the case that they could sit and have a detached, impersonal conversation about where their relationship was headed. He shook his head: what would be the point of detached and impersonal? That was the last thing he wanted. It had taken Eva to show him how stunted that had left his life. How much he was missing out on.

He wanted this to be personal, and he didn't care if it got messy. He didn't care if he got hurt. He just wanted it to be real.

'Have a seat. I'll get us a drink,' he said, heading for the kitchen and buying himself a couple of minutes to decide what he wanted to say first.

He thought back to what his dad had said to him about how he should tell her what he felt. How he had been able to see through the complications of their relationship to the fact that they cared about each other. And he was right. Whatever else was fake about their relationship, the feelings he had for her—the strength he felt from knowing he had her support—that was real.

He hoped it was for her too.

He brought two gin and tonics through and set them on the table, taking a seat opposite Eva, noticing how the shine of the waves in her hair caught and played in the candlelight.

'Did you sleep?' Eva asked. 'You look better.'

'Yeah, I did, thanks. I feel it. Everything okay in the office?'

She looked slightly disappointed at the question, and he could understand why. He was disappointed in himself for asking it. He didn't want small talk. He wanted more than that. He wanted to talk about them: what they were to each other and where they were going.

'Everything's fine. Any news from your dad?'

'He's fine too. Look, Eva, this afternoon you asked me to think. And I have. Since I left the office I've done nothing *but* think. About you.'

She gave a small nod and lifted her brows, encouraging him to go on.

'And you're right. I've been scared. Scared of history repeating itself. Scared of hurting you. When I left you alone the other night I knew what I was doing. I don't think I get a free pass on that just because Dad is sick.'

'I didn't say anything about a free pass,' Eva said, her voice steadier than his. 'Yes, you hurt me. I expect you to learn from that. And to try extremely hard not to do it again.'

'Did it make you think of your parents?' Joss asked.

It wasn't where he'd planned on this conversation going, but he was curious. Something about her had changed in the days that he'd been at the hospital with his dad, and he wanted to understand her better.

Eva nodded. 'Of course it did. But knowing what you were going through with your dad also made me think harder about them than I have before. When I was a teenager the "poor abandoned me" routine was easier to maintain. But I'm an adult now, and I don't expect the world to revolve around me. There are other things going on, and lots of interests that compete with mine. I want to be with someone who makes me a priority. But I'd rather be alone than with someone who doesn't put the needs of their sick parent above mine. My parents did what they thought was right: they lived trying to balance all of the lives they felt were their responsibility. And for them the lives of people caught up in conflict were just as important as mine. They protected me from the effects of that as much as they could, and I never gave them credit for it. I think they genuinely did the best they could, and it wouldn't be fair of me to expect more than that of them.'

Joss leaned back in his chair and took a sip of his drink. So *that* was what had changed. 'That's quite a realisation to come to after so many years.'

'Yeah, well, I had a bit of a push.' She gave him a meaningful look. 'And a weekend with nothing to do but think.'

He leaned forward and reached across the table for Eva's hand. When she turned her palm to meet his and threaded their fingers together he couldn't hold back the smile that spread across his features.

'Eva, you said earlier that you want to try loving me. Well, I want that too. I want you to try desperately hard—because I'm already so in love with you. I want to be with you, here, every day for the rest of our lives. I want to feel *this* ring...' he turned their hands over and kissed the diamonds they had chosen together '...every time I hold your hand, and remember how I felt the day we chose it. How I feel right this second.'

He paused, and looked up from her hand to meet her gaze.

'I want to hear you say I love you in every language you know. I want you to teach me to say it back, so that I'm never lost for a way to tell you exactly how I feel. I want you to be my wife, Eva.'

Her hand gripped his a little harder, and he knew he

had taken her by surprise. Well, no wonder. He'd surprised himself. He already knew he wanted to be with her, but he hadn't planned to ask that question just yet. Now that it was out there, he realised how desperate he was for her to feel the same. He looked into her eyes, tried to read her answer from the shape of her mouth, the expression in her eyes.

'Yes,' she said eventually, a smile breaking her features at last. 'Yes,' she said again as she rose from the table and took a step towards him. *'Oui.'*

At the sight of her pursed lips and the sound of those breathy vowels, he ached to pull her into his lap, but she wasn't done yet.

'Sí, sì, naí, ja,' she added as she reached him, and placed a hand on each of his cheeks.

She leaned in close, so close he could have met her lips with the tiniest movement. But this moment was all hers, and he wanted to hear her tell him yes in every language she could.

'Ano, tak, ie, na'am. I love you, Joss. Of course I'll marry you.'

At last her lips met his, and heat swept through him as he pulled her into his lap, threaded his fingers through her hair and kissed her with all the passion he'd been holding back for weeks. Part of him—no surprise which part—wanted to pick her up, carry her to the bedroom and never let her go. But there was more to this than just wanting her.

'I love you,' he told her again as he wrapped his arms tight around her waist, holding her hard against him.

'I've never wanted anything more than I want to make you happy and to deserve you.'

She smiled down at him, and he felt the connection that ran between them pull at him deep inside.

'We're going to work so hard to deserve each other,' she said with a smile. 'Every day. For the rest of our lives.'

He tipped her face down to his, and poured his whole heart into their kiss.

* * * * *

If you enjoyed this story, then don't miss
FALLING FOR THE REBEL PRINCESS
by Ellie Darkins
Available now!

If you want to indulge in another feel-good romance,
then make sure to treat yourself to
A PROPOSAL FROM THE ITALIAN COUNT
by Lucy Gordon

MILLS & BOON®
Hardback – September 2017

ROMANCE

The Tycoon's Outrageous Proposal	Miranda Lee
Cipriani's Innocent Captive	Cathy Williams
Claiming His One-Night Baby	Michelle Smart
At the Ruthless Billionaire's Command	Carole Mortimer
Engaged for Her Enemy's Heir	Kate Hewitt
His Drakon Runaway Bride	Tara Pammi
The Throne He Must Take	Chantelle Shaw
The Italian's Virgin Acquisition	Michelle Conder
A Proposal from the Crown Prince	Jessica Gilmore
Sarah and the Secret Sheikh	Michelle Douglas
Conveniently Engaged to the Boss	Ellie Darkins
Her New York Billionaire	Andrea Bolter
The Doctor's Forbidden Temptation	Tina Beckett
From Passion to Pregnancy	Tina Beckett
The Midwife's Longed-For Baby	Caroline Anderson
One Night That Changed Her Life	Emily Forbes
The Prince's Cinderella Bride	Amalie Berlin
Bride for the Single Dad	Jennifer Taylor
A Family for the Billionaire	Dani Wade
Taking Home the Tycoon	Catherine Mann

MILLS & BOON®
Large Print – September 2017

ROMANCE

The Sheikh's Bought Wife	Sharon Kendrick
The Innocent's Shameful Secret	Sara Craven
The Magnate's Tempestuous Marriage	Miranda Lee
The Forced Bride of Alazar	Kate Hewitt
Bound by the Sultan's Baby	Carol Marinelli
Blackmailed Down the Aisle	Louise Fuller
Di Marcello's Secret Son	Rachael Thomas
Conveniently Wed to the Greek	Kandy Shepherd
His Shy Cinderella	Kate Hardy
Falling for the Rebel Princess	Ellie Darkins
Claimed by the Wealthy Magnate	Nina Milne

HISTORICAL

The Secret Marriage Pact	Georgie Lee
A Warriner to Protect Her	Virginia Heath
Claiming His Defiant Miss	Bronwyn Scott
Rumours at Court (Rumors at Court)	Blythe Gifford
The Duke's Unexpected Bride	Lara Temple

MEDICAL

Their Secret Royal Baby	Carol Marinelli
Her Hot Highland Doc	Annie O'Neil
His Pregnant Royal Bride	Amy Ruttan
Baby Surprise for the Doctor Prince	Robin Gianna
Resisting Her Army Doc Rival	Sue MacKay
A Month to Marry the Midwife	Fiona McArthur

MILLS & BOON®
Hardback – October 2017

ROMANCE

Claimed for the Leonelli Legacy	Lynne Graham
The Italian's Pregnant Prisoner	Maisey Yates
Buying His Bride of Convenience	Michelle Smart
The Tycoon's Marriage Deal	Melanie Milburne
Undone by the Billionaire Duke	Caitlin Crews
His Majesty's Temporary Bride	Annie West
Bound by the Millionaire's Ring	Dani Collins
The Virgin's Shock Baby	Heidi Rice
Whisked Away by Her Sicilian Boss	Rebecca Winters
The Sheikh's Pregnant Bride	Jessica Gilmore
A Proposal from the Italian Count	Lucy Gordon
Claiming His Secret Royal Heir	Nina Milne
Sleigh Ride with the Single Dad	Alison Roberts
A Firefighter in Her Stocking	Janice Lynn
A Christmas Miracle	Amy Andrews
Reunited with Her Surgeon Prince	Marion Lennox
Falling for Her Fake Fiancé	Sue MacKay
The Family She's Longed For	Lucy Clark
Billionaire Boss, Holiday Baby	Janice Maynard
Billionaire's Baby Bind	Katherine Garbera

MILLS & BOON®
Large Print – October 2017

ROMANCE

Sold for the Greek's Heir	Lynne Graham
The Prince's Captive Virgin	Maisey Yates
The Secret Sanchez Heir	Cathy Williams
The Prince's Nine-Month Scandal	Caitlin Crews
Her Sinful Secret	Jane Porter
The Drakon Baby Bargain	Tara Pammi
Xenakis's Convenient Bride	Dani Collins
Her Pregnancy Bombshell	Liz Fielding
Married for His Secret Heir	Jennifer Faye
Behind the Billionaire's Guarded Heart	Leah Ashton
A Marriage Worth Saving	Therese Beharrie

HISTORICAL

The Debutante's Daring Proposal	Annie Burrows
The Convenient Felstone Marriage	Jenni Fletcher
An Unexpected Countess	Laurie Benson
Claiming His Highland Bride	Terri Brisbin
Marrying the Rebellious Miss	Bronwyn Scott

MEDICAL

Their One Night Baby	Carol Marinelli
Forbidden to the Playboy Surgeon	Fiona Lowe
A Mother to Make a Family	Emily Forbes
The Nurse's Baby Secret	Janice Lynn
The Boss Who Stole Her Heart	Jennifer Taylor
Reunited by Their Pregnancy Surprise	Louisa Heaton

MILLS & BOON®

Why shop at millsandboon.co.uk?

Each year, thousands of romance readers find their perfect read at millsandboon.co.uk. That's because we're passionate about bringing you the very best romantic fiction. Here are some of the advantages of shopping at www.millsandboon.co.uk:

* **Get new books first**—you'll be able to buy your favourite books one month before they hit the shops

* **Get exclusive discounts**—you'll also be able to buy our specially created monthly collections, with up to 50% off the RRP

* **Find your favourite authors**—latest news, interviews and new releases for all your favourite authors and series on our website, plus ideas for what to try next

* **Join in**—once you've bought your favourite books, don't forget to register with us to rate, review and join in the discussions

Visit **www.millsandboon.co.uk**
for all this and more today!